LIVE
FROM BRENTWOOD HIGH

Double
Danger

Cedar River Daydreams

Live! From Brentwood High

Other Books by Judy Baer

LIVE
FROM BRENTWOOD HIGH

Double Danger

JUDY BAER

BETHANY HOUSE PUBLISHERS
MINNEAPOLIS, MINNESOTA 55438

Double Danger
Judy Baer

Cover illustration by Joe Nordstrom

Library of Congress Catalog Card Number
Applied For

ISBN 1–55661–388–1

Copyright © 1994
Judy Baer

Published by Bethany House Publishers
A Ministry of Bethany Fellowship, Inc.
11300 Hampshire Avenue South
Minneapolis, Minnesota 55438

Printed in the United States of America

For Adrienne, her roommate, and friends at Concordia—to cheer you up and to cheer you on!

LIVE

FROM BRENTWOOD HIGH

PROLOGUE

LIVE

FROM BRENTWOOD HIGH

"I'm gonna tear your heart out, you little toad!"

"Try it. You'll regret it."

"Maybe you don't even have a heart inside that thing you call a body...."

The threats and jibes escalated quickly and bitterly, along with the pushing, shoving, and taunts of the bystanders. Suddenly, a knife appeared and instantly smothered the jeers. Only the squeak of rubber-soled tennis shoes against cold tile and the hiss of a blade broke the silence.

A gasp, then a scream filled the air, and the crowd evaporated like a mist.

"Chaos Central" buzzed with activity as the *Live! From Brentwood High* staff raced to meet their deadlines. Joshua Willis pounded two-fingered on an old typewriter balanced on a battered school desk. He had two pencils and a plastic straw stuck behind one ear; a large rubber band draped the other. A wadded spitball was lodged in his kinky black hair. To maintain his concentration as he typed, Josh chewed on his tongue. At the moment, he appeared to be in danger of chewing it off entirely.

Sarah Riley wedged her wheelchair between Andrew Tremaine and Molly Ashton as they sat at a long, narrow table editing sections of script to be used for the next newscast. Molly pulled thoughtfully at the curly blond frizz of her hair and chewed on the eraser tip of her pencil while Jake Saunders and Darby Ellison paced in opposite directions, practicing their introductions for an upcoming story.

Julie Osborn, Kate Akima, and Shane Donahue sat near the windows, catching rays and reading the material their instructor and supervisor, Ms. Rosie Wright, had assigned. Others from the staff moved around the room in the brisk, businesslike fashion everyone instinctively adopted when they entered the newsroom.

Located in the halls of Brentwood High School, the media room housed juniors and seniors in the television production class for the student-run cable television station. *Live! From Brentwood High!* aired schoolwide, and on Saturday nights a ninety-second feature story produced by the students ran on the local news station. As Izzy Mooney, the class clown *and* class sage, often commented, "This is *real*, dudes, so don't blow it!"

Ms. Wright and her assistant Gary Richmond entered, carrying large boxes of books and video tapes. Ms. Wright's heels thunked noisily against the tile floor as she walked. As usual, she was dressed in an eclectic hodge-podge—cranberry-colored broomstick skirt, black bodysuit, and cowboy boots—that would have looked strange on anyone but her.

Gary, too, had his own style of dressing. It consisted of worn jeans, a multipocketed khaki jacket, and a decrepit T-shirt. His brown hair was pulled back into a shaggy ponytail.

As they entered, Josh's brown eyes lit with relief. "There you are! I've got a question about this—"

He was interrupted by a sharp bark of dismay. Shane leaped to his feet and lunged toward the window. The chair in which he'd been sitting skittered three feet before falling sideways against a bookcase.

"What's going on out there?" Shane pressed so close to the window that his nose flattened at the tip.

The students stared in amazement. Shane *never*

got excited about anything. He rarely registered any expression other than disinterest or a knowing sneer. It didn't fit his macho, tough-guy image. To see him squashed against a plate-glass window was catalyst enough to propel everyone to the window. Even Gary and Ms. Wright hurried to see what had inspired Shane's interest.

The street outside the school was swarming with emergency vehicles. Flashing red lights from police cars, ambulances, and fire department rescue vehicles winked in the sunlight.

"Must have been a traffic accident," Julie speculated.

"A *big* one."

"Then where's the accident?" Josh wondered aloud. "And why didn't we hear the crash?"

As the chaos below them sorted itself out, two police vehicles pulled out of the way and an ambulance backed slowly up the sidewalk toward the main door of the school.

"They're coming in *here*!" Julie squealed. "Something's happened inside the school!"

At that moment, the door to the media room opened and slammed shut again. Isador Eugene Mooney collapsed against the far wall, white as a bed sheet. Pearly beads of sweat had collected on his upper lip. His hedge of always uncontrolled hair was literally standing on end. There seemed to be a distinct possibility that Izzy was about to faint.

Jake swung over the top of a table and reached Izzy just as the large boy's knees buckled. Jake jammed his shoulder beneath one of Izzy's arms and propped him up as Izzy's feet began to slide out from under him.

"Don't faint on me, Izz," Jake advised. "You're too big to pick up."

Josh, who'd realized what was happening almost as quickly as Jake, took Izzy's other arm. Between them, they steered Izzy toward a chair. He could barely lift one high-top clad foot in front of the other.

"You look like *you* should be in that ambulance," Darby observed wryly. "What in the world happened?"

Izzy's weak stomach and low tolerance for anything resembling blood or bodily functions were directly opposite in proportion to his size and appearance. Large and tough as Izzy looked, he had a reputation for fainting regularly in biology class. Now Izzy was gulping great breaths of air.

Gary dropped to his knees in front of Izzy. "You're shaking like a leaf. Slow down or you're going to hyperventilate. If you faint, it would take a crane to hoist you off the floor."

He put two fingers on Izzy's wrist. "Your pulse is racing. Do you need a doctor?"

"Doctor? No way! Keep them away from me!"

"Isador, you're the only one who seems to know what's going on. You'd better tell us." Ms. Wright could sound very fierce—especially when she was upset.

"I was in the—uh—west wing of the school," Izzy stammered, his color and his breath coming back to him in increments. "I heard there was leftover food in the home ec. department and . . ."

"We understand. You were hungry. As usual. Keep going," Darby prodded.

"The only things left were doughnuts and carrot cake, so I asked if I could bring some back to the media room. They gave me a whole pan of stuff. . . ." Izzy dazedly looked around, realizing for the first time that he'd misplaced his food along the way. "And there were some guys fighting . . ."

"Fighting? Slow down, Izz. Who was fighting?"

"I didn't recognize most of them. Sophomores, I think. Younger kids. Two guys were doing the actual shoving and pushing. The others had taken sides and were taunting each other. It was weird. Really mean and vicious. I've seen fights in school before but nothing like this. . . ."

"Were they wearing colors?" Shane asked.

Gary's head snapped up at Shane's question. "*Gang* colors?"

Shane's already dark expression deepened. "Maybe."

"Why haven't I heard about this?" Gary's question was staccato sharp. "Are there organized gangs in Brentwood?"

"There *were* colors," Izzy muttered, oblivious to the conversation between Gary and Shane. "I remember now. Several of the guys were wearing yellow bandannas. I *thought* it was weird. . . ."

"What about the others?"

"A lot of them wore green baseball caps."

Shane's sharp intake of breath indicated that whatever Izzy had seen was indeed gang related. Specific colors were worn by gang members as means of both identification and intimidation. Wearing colors was also an invitation to fight—or a nonverbal order for others to leave the area.

"I didn't realize we had active gangs in Brentwood!" Kate blurted. "We're not that kind of school!"

Shane looked pityingly at Kate. "They've been here all along. You just didn't notice because you didn't *want* to notice. Come out of your dreamworld, Kate—and meet reality."

"Is any school free of violence these days?" Ms. Wright sounded as though she were thinking out loud. "Izzy, tell us what else you saw."

"Two guys were pushing, shoving, and calling each other names. They both kept insisting that the other guy was on their territory. The fight kept getting worse for no reason." Izzy's expression was baffled. "It was as if these guys hated each other just for *existing*.

"There was a lot of cussing and screaming. The others were chanting something that I couldn't quite catch. I only knew that I was someplace I didn't want to be and that I'd better get out of there fast. I don't know where all the teachers and hall monitors were. Hiding, maybe. If it were up to me to break up a fight like that, I know I would have hidden."

"Then what happened?"

"The boy in the green cap pulled something out of his pocket. At first I thought it was a pen. It was silver—like the one you use sometimes, Ms. Wright."

Izzy's color had finally returned.

"It wasn't until the kid in green jammed it into the other guy's chest that I realized it was a knife." Izzy lifted his hands and held two fingers several inches apart. "I'd never seen a switchblade before . . . but I think I have now."

Izzy's head slumped toward his chest. "I think it went through his heart."

Molly gasped and burst into tears.

Izzy swallowed thickly and ran a shaky hand through his buzzed-off hair. "There was blood everywhere. The kid who was stabbed slid to the floor. The other guy reached down, pulled out the knife and wiped the blade on the hurt guy's pant leg—calm as could be. Just like he stabbed people every day. The guys in green were cheering and laughing.

"That's when two teachers walked into the hall. All of a sudden, everybody vanished—including me. I stopped at the office and told someone to call an ambulance, but someone had already reported it."

Big, hulking Izzy buried his face in his hands and burst into tears. "I think I just saw somebody get killed."

Gary moved toward the door. "I want you to *stay here*. I'll find out what's going on. I don't want any of you rushing down the hall and getting in the way. Understand?"

The shocked students nodded dumbly. While Ms. Wright stayed by Izzy, talking low into his ear, Kate and Julie returned to the window.

"They're bringing someone out on a stretcher!" Julie said. "I can't see the face. It must be the guy Izzy saw. . . ."

"Look! The paramedics are giving him oxygen." Kate's voice betrayed a strange excitement.

"The first ambulance looks like it's ready to pull away."

As Kate and Julie gave a play-by-play of the scene outside the window, the others stayed where they were, trying to comprehend what had happened.

Only Shane did not seem completely blown away by the turn of events.

"They've got a kid in handcuffs!" Kate squealed. "I wish he'd turn around so I could see his face! Do you think it's anybody we know?"

"Now the other vehicles are leaving." Julie sounded disappointed. "It must be over."

"Can you believe it? A stabbing at our school!"

"Other junk happens. Why not a stabbing?"

"What other junk?" There were always stories, but in a school this size, who listened?

"Stealing. Fighting. Don't you remember last spring when five kids got expelled for having a fight with baseball bats in the parking lot?"

"I heard about two guys who went after each other with chains." Julie savored the gossip. "One guy got his cheekbone crushed before the teachers stopped it.

"And there's a *reason* they don't allow us to use padlocks on our gym lockers anymore. Some kids were using them to fight with," Julie continued.

"My uncle is a policeman," Jake said, walking over to the window. "He says most of the gang trouble around here is a small, hard-core group. Lots of kids have joined, but only a few get into the violence."

"Then why do they join?"

"To be part of a group, I suppose. Everybody

wants friends. Young kids get into it because they see the older ones doing it and think it looks tough. Older ones get into it because they enjoy bossing others around or like the thrill of doing something wrong."

"I didn't know . . ." Darby was shocked. She turned to Sarah and Molly. "Did you?"

Sarah looked deeply troubled. "No. But then no member of a gang would ever be interested in talking to me." She patted the arm of her wheelchair.

"They'd be afraid you'd try to convert 'em," Julie pointed out bluntly, referring to Sarah's faith. The *Live!* staff was just beginning to appreciate what it meant for Sarah to be a Christian.

"Looks like they need converting," Molly said. "What's wrong with these people anyway? Baseball bats? Chains? Knives? Gangs? In our school? Why is it happening here?"

"Why is it happening anywhere?" Shane was the least verbal member of the group, so whenever he spoke, the rest listened. "Because it's nice to know someone's watching your back," he said bluntly. "Acceptance. Safety."

"I'd hardly consider getting stabbed in the heart *safe*," Josh muttered.

"Everybody needs to belong somewhere," Sarah said. "Maybe that's what they're looking for—someone to trust, someone to care about them. That's what Shane means. People who join gangs want to belong to someone."

"Brentwood's a nice place," Molly said. "The people are good citizens. It's the sort of thing that happens other places, but not in *my hometown!*"

"Believe it," Shane said shortly. "You just haven't been around to see it."

"And you have?"

The room grew still. Where Shane spent his time after school was a mystery. They knew very little of his background. It was obvious that he knew what he was talking about—but *how* did he know? Shane stared at the toes of his boots without speaking.

Finally, he lifted his head. "My cousin was shot to death by a gang member when she was sixteen years old." His voice sounded tinny and distant.

"Here?" Darby asked.

"No. In Los Angeles. She was dating a guy she'd met after her family moved to L.A. She came from a little town in Georgia and didn't know much about city life. She didn't even know gangs existed.

"When she broke up with this guy to date someone else, she didn't worry about his being upset. She thought he'd get over it. That's how it worked back home, she said.

"But he didn't get over it. Once he found out that she was dating a guy associated with an opposing gang, he went ballistic. When she ignored his threats, he went to her house and shot her."

"Oh, Shane, I'm so sorry." Sarah's gentle eyes filled with tears.

Shane, who rarely smiled for anyone, smiled crookedly at Sarah.

"I'm *bummed*!" Molly announced. "Is everybody going crazy or what?"

The others nodded somberly but said nothing.

Izzy's deep, ragged breathing could be heard throughout the room.

Suddenly Molly slapped the palms of her hands onto the table and stood up. Her eyes were shining and a wide, incredulous smile split her features. "Do any of you realize what we're sitting on here?"

"A disaster," Josh muttered.

"The end of freedom in this school," Julie offered. "Imagine how many rules and regulations we're going to have to follow now!"

"The end of *safety*," Darby added sadly. "I never thought this could happen here."

"That's it!" Molly crowed.

"And you're happy about it?" Kate gave Molly a sour look.

"Of course not. Do you think I'm crazy? But while we're sitting here moaning and wailing about what's happened, we aren't taking into account that school violence is one of the biggest issues facing teenagers today!"

"So what? Sometimes it's not so great being part of the majority. Especially not when . . ." Jake's voice trailed away.

" . . . especially not when it affects you personally!" Darby jumped up from her chair and reached for Molly's arm.

"What are you talking about?" Julie grumbled.

"We're experiencing a national phenomenon firsthand—violence in school!"

"Big deal. Who wants . . ." Then it was as though a light flicked on inside Julie's head. And Josh's. And Sarah's.

"This is a story for *Live!*"

"Can we do it? It will be pretty tough."

"We can't ignore it. Izzy *saw* the stabbing! The personal aspects are what will give the story its punch. There isn't a more powerful story than that."

They were off and running, brainstorming ideas and angles, drawing up lists of teachers, students, and police to interview. It took a moment for anyone to hear Ms. Wright noisily clearing her throat. "Does anyone have anything they'd like to say to me?"

"Oh!" Molly blushed a rosy pink. "We forgot. Ms. Wright, do you think a story on violence in schools is a good one for the *Live!* staff to cover?"

Rosie looked amused. "I think it's a *great* idea. The school will have to deal with this problem anyway. Whatever knowledge you students can gather and disseminate will be helpful and timely. Besides, I want to congratulate you all. It's wonderful to see you taking the initiative."

Ms. Wright started to point at the students with the ruler in her hand.

"Darby, Izzy, Julie, Sarah—I want you to take responsibility for this story even though I'd like everyone to do research and have input. And, Shane, I'd like you to be on this team also. You'll bring an added dimension to the story."

"He knows all about gangs, you mean," Kate muttered under her breath. "He probably belongs to one."

Though Kate's words were soft and muffled, Shane lifted his head to look at her. There was a glint of steel in his blue-gray eyes, a warning that said Shane knew plenty he was not willing to share.

Ms. Wright clapped her hands and gave everyone an encouraging grin. The awkward moment was shattered. "What are you waiting for? Get busy! This crew may make a news team yet!"

CHAPTER 2

LIVE

FROM BRENTWOOD HIGH

Until now Brentwood High had escaped the serious violence that plagued neighboring schools. Word of the stabbing spread rapidly throughout the school and community. With each retelling, the story became a little wilder and more graphic, until even Izzy was forced to correct the misstatements and exaggerations attaching themselves to the event. If one listened to the gossip, it appeared that Brentwood had turned from a peaceful, upscale community into a war zone.

———

"Have you heard the latest?" Julie's excited question preceded her into the media room.

"Now what?" Izzy looked tired. His fuzzy hair was flattened on one side, his clothes were seriously rumpled, and there were dark circles under his eyes.

Julie eyed him speculatively. "What's wrong with you, bed head?"

"You're only the forty-millionth one to ask." Izzy scowled.

"Didn't sleep, huh?"

"*Couldn't* sleep is more like it. I kept seeing that kid lying there with that black-red blood bubbling up out of his chest...."

"That settles it! Isador, you're going to the counselor's office this afternoon, like it or not."

"I'm all right, Ms. Wright. I just couldn't turn my brain off last night...."

"Izzy, you saw something dreadful happen. You can't expect to get over it"—she snapped her fingers—"just like that. And you can't always get over it alone. I'll arrange an appointment right now."

When Ms. Wright had left the room, Izzy raked his fingers through the stubble of his hair. "When am I going to learn to keep my mouth shut? If only I could turn off my brain, I'd be okay! But I keep seeing that kid lunge and the blood pooling on the other guy's chest. There I was, frozen to the spot, useless. Useless! I watched a kid die and could do nothing about it. I wish I could forget...."

"You can't forget, Izzy, no matter how hard you try. Just like you aren't going to get by without talking to a counselor," Julie told him. "That's part of my news. The school has invited crisis counselors to talk to us about what happened yesterday."

"What's the rest of your news?" Kate enjoyed excitement and juicy gossip as much as Julie did. The stabbing had provided plenty of both.

"Some parents have pulled their kids out of school! There's a line down the hall at the administration office and some of the parents are *furious*. They're saying things like 'unsafe environment' and 'bad influences for our children.'"

"But where will those kids go?" Sarah wondered aloud.

"I asked around. Some of them have already been enrolled in private schools. Others are going to be home-schooled until this stabbing thing gets straightened out."

Andrew Tremaine snorted loudly. "Big help that's going to be! Running away never solved anything. Those parents are trying to get away from the problem rather than face it."

"Funny, Andrew, but I think you've been guilty of the same thing a time or two." Molly put her hands on her hips and glared at him.

Andrew had been one who'd denied that the problem of sexual harassment existed even after Molly had admitted being harassed at her after-school job as a waitress. This switch to the high road came as something of a surprise to them all.

"I'm not sure it's running away," Darby said. "If I thought my child wasn't safe, I'd be tempted to remove him or her from the situation."

"Why not remove the gangs instead?" Sarah asked. "It's *our* school too. Why should the well-behaved kids have to suffer?"

"That's a pretty interesting question," Jake commented. "I hear a lot of the kids involved in yesterday's 'altercation' have convenient cases of memory lapse. They can't even remember being in the hallway when it happened."

"And all those colored bandannas and caps Izzy saw?"

"Gone. Just like they never existed."

"In other words, it's going to be difficult to discover who was really involved?"

"Exactly. They've got the kid who was stabbed and the one who did it. The others cheering them on are trying to become invisible."

"My parents didn't want me to come to school today," Kate admitted.

"And my dad kept saying, 'What's the world coming to?'" Josh quoted. "I don't think anybody was happy about coming."

"Well, it makes me mad!" Molly's frizzy blond hair bounced around her face. She appeared both agitated and indignant. "It's not *fair!* Why do people act like this? It's ruined our school!"

"The school isn't ruined yet," Sarah pointed out. "And it doesn't have to be if this is handled correctly."

"Brentwood's reputation has always been good. Now we're going to be known as just another school with gang fights!"

"I don't feel safe here anymore," Molly complained. "It used to be comfortable to go to school here. Now it's . . . scary. If stuff like this could happen *here*, it could happen anywhere!"

As usual, they'd all forgotten Gary was present until he cleared his throat. He had a chameleonlike way of disappearing into the background. He rarely spoke unless he had something important to say.

"Your feelings are all perfectly normal," he said calmly. "In fact, it would be unusual if you *didn't* feel fear, shock, anger, or resentment. That's why the counselors are coming—to help you work through those feelings."

"I suppose we could use it in our story," Jake said matter-of-factly, looking for the bright side. "No use wasting good material."

"Actually, researching and writing the story might *be* a good way to work through your feelings," Gary said. "Lots of times I've used my own pain to film a better story."

Gary did not often refer to his life as a photographer and photojournalist before he'd come to Brentwood. He'd worked with news teams for national television, traveling from story to story and crisis to crisis at the expense of his personal life. It was strangely comforting to know that Gary thought this could be worked through.

"What do the teachers think about this?" Kate wondered aloud. "Have they said anything?"

Gary shrugged. He didn't hang around the teachers' lounge. He was usually firmly planted in the media room. "Most of the talk I've heard has been about gun control."

"But there weren't any guns involved."

"It's not a very far step from stabbing someone with a knife to shooting them with a gun. If that kid had had a gun in his pocket instead of a knife, two or three students might have been dead right now."

Izzy looked even more glum. "It could have been me!"

"Aren't you exaggerating just a little?" Andrew asked.

"The assassinations of President John F. Kennedy, Senator Robert Kennedy, and Reverend Martin Luther King Jr. made our country take a hard look at gun control. Some of the brightest leaders in our country died because madmen carried handguns," Gary commented, ignoring Andrew.

"So what are people doing about this?" Molly propped her fists on her hips and glared at Gary as if he were personally responsible for the entire older generation.

"Policies have been tried. Some states require background checks for people who purchase guns. That prevents those with criminal records from buying guns. The Brady Bill requires a waiting period for handgun purchases."

"What good does that do?"

"It's a cooling-off period, I suppose. It stops people from committing crimes in the heat of passion by forcing them to wait a few days to purchase a gun."

"But that doesn't help people who *plan* their crimes."

"I think they should put criminals in jail and throw away the key," Kate crossed her arms for emphasis. "*All* of them!"

"What's that going to fix? Let's get rid of the guns instead. Make the laws tougher."

"How about just enforcing the laws we already have?"

The argument went round and round.

"There are lots of guns floating around. It can't be that hard to get one—even for kids."

"That's why this incident is so upsetting," Darby interjected. "It's not a story on the national news anymore. It's *our* story."

"I wish we'd get some details," Julie complained.

"The kids are all talking, but as far as I can tell, the adults are trying to sweep this under the rug."

"Maybe not." Ms. Wright entered the room. "There'll be an announcement over the intercom soon. There's to be an assembly this afternoon. If you want to know what the administration plans to do, that's the place to be."

Izzy snapped out of his morose reverie. "Could we take the ENG camera down to film the meeting? I could do it alone if you're busy, Gary. Even though I haven't taken it on location yet, I know I could manage to tape something in the gym."

Gary glanced at Rosie Wright. "What do you think?"

"It's not a bad idea. These kids have a report to put together. There might be relevant information offered that we'd like on tape. I know the administration is open to everyone's input, including ours at *Live!*"

"Okay. Come with me, Izz. We'll make sure everything is ready to go."

As Izzy and Gary wandered off, deep in technical discussion about cameras, Jake walked over to Darby and put his hand on her shoulder.

"Uptight?"

"Very. I can't get this out of my mind."

"Maybe you shouldn't try. Sometimes you have to face your fears in order to conquer them. I think Gary's right. Doing a story on violence will help us sort out what's most frightening."

"Does this ever get to you?" Darby asked as she rolled her head to the right and to the left, allowing the muscles to relax. "The pressure, I mean."

"Not really. Why? Does it bother you?"

"Sometimes. And it scares me. What if I can't do it, Jake? What if I get too personally involved in every story? What if I'm not cut out to do the one thing I've wanted to do my entire life?"

"Don't worry, Darby. If you care enough about something you'll find a way to do it. That's what my dad always says. I think in ten years you'll be reporting the news somewhere, just like Anna Leemon does here in Brentwood."

"And what will *you* be doing?"

"I don't know. I wish I did. I'd like to be focused like you are. Sometimes I'm afraid I'll drift too long."

"You've got plenty of time. Just think about what you're good at and then decide what you should be."

"I'm good at sports, chemistry, and handling a houseful of women," Jake said, referring to his four older sisters. "What does that qualify me to do?"

"Go into sports medicine for female athletes?"

He burst out laughing. "Quick thinking, Darby. That's what I like about you." His smile focused on her. "And I like you a lot."

"Ms. Wright wouldn't like to hear you say that."

"Ms. Wright can't regulate every part of our lives—even though that's what she may want."

"According to Ms. Wright, 'Business and pleasure don't mix.' "

"All work and no play makes Jake a dull boy," he retorted. "Besides, there'll be lots of romances in the *Live!* staff before the year is out."

"Like who?"

"Andrew and Molly, for one."

"No way! Molly hates him. She calls him a lazy slug and the most conceited boy on the planet."

"She's crazy about him."

"She is not!"

"Then she will be. Haven't you noticed how well behaved Andrew has become around Molly?"

"Well behaved? Is that what it is with him? I thought maybe he wasn't feeling well."

"Very funny. Andrew is trying. I know. I can tell. He's mellowing."

"I hope he isn't setting himself up for a fall," Darby said. "I'm not sure if Molly is completely over her old boyfriend—and I know she doesn't like Andrew. If that blows up, it's going to make working with the *Live!* staff pretty miserable."

"And Ms. Wright will tell everyone 'I told you so.'"

Darby sighed and stood up. "Don't you hate it? Parents and teachers usually *are* right!"

———

"Is this place tense or what?" Darby looked around the room full of unsmiling faces as she and Sarah entered the gymnasium. Even the school's most notorious goof-offs were subdued.

She took the handgrips of Sarah's wheelchair and steered her to a spot at the end of the bleachers. They had to pass two armed policemen to reach their destination.

"This looks more like a prison than a school." Molly glared at the blank, expressionless faces of the guards. "Why'd they have to bring *them* in?"

"Better to be safe than sorry, I guess. I suppose they don't want more trouble."

"Oh, Sarah, you're too accepting. I hate it that my school has to have guards!"

Molly wasn't the only one, judging by the comments from the other students. Everyone was edgy. Nervous laughter and weak jokes skittered across the room like rocks skipping on a still pond.

"What do you get when you mix greens and yellows together?"

"I dunno. Blue, I suppose."

"Nope. Red. The color of blood. Green? Yellow? They make blood every time."

"That's a really sick joke."

"This is a really sick deal."

Darby tried not to listen. She hated what was happening to her school.

Molly jammed her in the ribs with her elbow. "Look! Even the school board is here!"

"How can you tell?" Julie dropped down next to them on a bleacher. "Have you ever seen them before?"

"Today. They had an emergency meeting this morning to decide what to do about the stabbing," Molly informed her. "I heard about it in the girls' bathroom."

"Well then, it *must* be true. No lies *ever* come out of there!"

"Quit it, you two," Sarah chided gently. "We've got enough trouble right now."

As Mr. Edward Black walked to the podium, si-

lence followed him. It was unheard of to have the
president of the school board address the students except on graduation day. That alone told everyone just
how much importance was placed on this meeting.

"By now all of you have heard of the tragic incident that took place in our school yesterday. In all the
years I've been involved with this school system,
nothing has shocked me like this unexpected eruption
of violence. Quite frankly, I am dismayed, disheart-
ened, and disappointed that any of our students could
be involved in such a tragedy."

"Give us a break," someone muttered. "We didn't
all do it!"

"In an emergency meeting held this morning, the
school board and administration have decided to immediately implement a 'No Coat' policy."

"Since when did coats become dangerous?"

"No more outerwear—jackets, coats, etcetera—
can be worn inside the school. They must be removed
when you enter and placed in your lockers. We realize
that this may be inconvenient, but because it is too
easy to conceal weapons in bulky outerwear, this re-
striction has become necessary."

"Fear of flannel? That's a new one!" Andrew
sneered.

"This rule will be *strictly* enforced."

The moans and mutterings of the student body indicated the lack of warmth with which this new rule
was received.

"Our board has also instituted another policy. . . ."

"Now what? A No Shoes policy? I suppose you

could club someone with a pair of wing tips," Andrew grumbled.

"From this time forward, the board and administration of Brentwood High have a 'Zero Tolerance' policy for weapons carried into the school building by students. Do not, and I repeat, *do not* bring any sort of weapon into this school. This includes guns, knives, scissors, brass knuckles, cap guns, chains, baseball bats, etcetera. If you do, even for benign reasons, *you will be suspended or possibly expelled*. Bringing those items onto school grounds is a violation of the zero tolerance weapons policy. I can promise you that anyone violating this rule will be dealt with swiftly."

Mr. Black glanced sharply at a cluster of boys near the back of the bleachers who were shifting restlessly and making remarks to one another. "For those of you who might consider taking this lightly, remember, *we will not tolerate violence in this school*. It is our responsibility to make this a secure place. The pledge we've made to your parents is that you will be safe within the walls of this building. Without safety, an atmosphere of learning cannot exist.

"Today, a letter explaining our new policies will go out to your parents. If they have questions, I invite them to the public meeting we are holding to discuss the new policies.

"I have nothing else to say other than this: We will not allow our school to become a battleground. These rules will be enforced with no exceptions. We already have the names of several of the students who were involved in yesterday's altercation and will investigate until we have them all. We're serious, ladies and gentlemen, and you'd better be serious too."

Jake and Darby walked out of the gym side by side. "Looks like things are going to tighten up around here."

"Sounds like a prison camp to me." Andrew sauntered up beside them. "I wonder when the barbed-wire fences are going up. Do you think they'll have guard dogs sniffing our clothes?"

Darby's first instinct was to chastise Andrew for being so negative, but she kept her mouth shut. For once, she almost agreed with him. It did feel like school had just turned into prison.

———

They were still discussing the assembly as several students gathered in the media room after school.

"I just bought the most awesome Western jacket with big pockets," Molly complained. "And now they tell me I can't wear it inside the school? Who do they think they are—the fashion police? I mean really. . . ."

"I think it's stupid," Julie added. "If somebody wants to get a weapon into this school, they'll get it in. What about purses and book bags? What about slipping a knife inside a boot? This isn't going to help anything."

"They've got to start somewhere," Sarah reminded the girls gently. "We'd be upset if they didn't do anything."

"Oh, Sarah, quit being such a goody-two-shoes. The administration is overreacting and you know it!" Kate jabbed a pencil into a mug already full of them.

"Pretty soon they'll have us marching to class and saluting teachers!"

"I think you're all being very unrealistic." Darby swung her legs back and forth as she sat on the edge of the bookshelves running the length of the room. "You're in denial. You don't want to believe this could happen here. That's why you're blaming the administration—because you don't want to accept the fact that this could happen again."

"When did you get to be a psychologist?" Kate asked. "At night school?"

"Much as I hate to agree with Julie and Kate," Andrew began, "I do. This once, at least. Things aren't as bad as everyone thinks they are. Until you can show me some proof that this is a trend and not an isolated incident, I don't think we should get excited."

"Doubting Thomas," Sarah accused softly.

"Huh?" Andrew spun to face her. "What does that mean?"

"You're being a doubting Thomas, that's all."

"I don't get it."

"Thomas was one of Jesus' disciples. He was the one who always questioned and doubted everything. He wouldn't even believe that Christ died on the cross and was resurrected until he personally saw the nail prints in His hands. Now someone who always demands proof before he will believe is called a doubting Thomas."

"Do you have to drag religion into everything, Sarah?"

Sarah grinned. "Yup. Especially now—because it's

relevant. Aren't journalists supposed to like what's relevant?"

"Okay, so tell us about Thomas."

"He needed physical proof—firsthand experience—in order to accept the information he was given about Christ's resurrection. You guys are doubters too—until you have solid physical proof that our administration needs to make the rules they have made. But it's okay to have doubts. Sometimes those doubts lead to questions and the questions inspire people to find answers. And that's good."

Sarah sat back in her wheelchair and folded her arms across her chest. "And that's my sermon for today."

For once, Julie, who usually poked fun at Sarah's slant on things, announced, "I agree."

Sarah looked startled at this strange turn of events.

"Sarah is right—about the doubts and questions part, at least. She's given me a wonderful idea!"

"I have?" Sarah wasn't accustomed to receiving either praise or approval from Julie.

"Sure. I think we should put together a survey on violence in schools. Does it exist or doesn't it? Are gangs on the increase or just a myth made up by nervous adults? Is violence *here* in our school or was the stabbing a freakish isolated incident? If violence is as prevalent as our school board thinks it is, then we'd better get some proof of it in order to convince kids to make some changes in their lifestyles. After all, we can't protect ourselves from something we don't even believe exists!"

"I agree with Julie," Andrew announced. "It's a great way to start the story for *Live!* We could be the first local group to gather this kind of information. Who knows? We might even get some extra attention from the media for this."

"Last ones out turn off the lights," Gary reminded them as he picked up his backpack and headed for the door. "By the way, I think you've come up with a great story. The administration might be very interested in what you learn in your survey. Keep up the good work and they could expand this program."

Jake grinned at Darby after Gary had left. "Hear that? Maybe we can get more credits."

"Ms. Wright would love more air time. Maybe, just maybe . . ."

"I don't know about the rest of you, but I'm sick of this." Julie picked up her books and purse and headed for the door. "Kate, let's go shopping."

"I need a break too. A movie, maybe. Or swimming." Jake turned to Darby. "Interested?"

All Darby's good intentions about keeping business and pleasure separate went out the window. Her mouth was in gear before her mind got out of neutral. "Sure."

"That sounds good to me too," Andrew said. "Would you mind if Molly and I joined you?"

It would have been hard to guess who looked more surprised—Jake, Darby, or Molly.

"I thought it might be fun if the four of us went together."

Molly stared at Andrew as if he'd just walked out of an alien spaceship. "You're asking *me* out?"

"Have you got a problem with that?"

"No, not exactly. I just never expected . . ."

Darby turned away so that Andrew could not see her face. Jake grinned and did the same. They'd have burst out laughing if they'd had to look at Molly for another second.

Though Molly had once admitted he was handsome—"in a reptilian sort of way"—she'd argued with and complained about Andrew more than any other guy in school.

Now, however, he'd caught her off guard. "I . . . uh . . . I . . . suppose so . . . maybe . . ."

Andrew had heard enough. "Great. What time should we pick the girls up, Jake? We could stop at my parents' restaurant, if anyone's interested."

Darby's eyes grew round. Figaro's was a very upscale place. This was suddenly no casual evening on the town.

Doubling with Andrew and Molly had just become serious business.

Figaro's was full, but when Andrew's father saw Darby, Jake, Molly, and Andrew at the door, he guided them to a private table in the far corner of the room and seated them with an elaborate flourish. Mr. Tremaine even pulled the cloth napkins out of the water goblets on the table and dropped them expertly into each lap.

"Your waiter will be here soon. Have fun, kids," he said as he walked off.

Molly's eyes were big as saucers. "Do you always get treatment like that?"

"Dad's in a good mood tonight. When I told him we were coming, he said he'd save us a table."

"He did a good job," Molly whispered in awe.

"This is my parents' table. They usually save it for themselves or special guests. It's the quietest and most secluded table in the restaurant. That makes it very desirable."

"And tonight they gave it to us." Molly was very impressed.

"It's busy tonight, so Mom and Dad won't take time to eat."

Jake looked at the menu the waiter had handed him and paled. "It's a good thing we came only for dessert. I don't have enough money in my checking account to pay for dinner here."

Darby opened her menu and understood what Jake had meant.

"Relax, you guys; it's my treat. After all, I get a discount." Andrew lifted a hand in the air and a waiter arrived immediately.

"Franco, would you please bring the dessert cart?"

"I'd be delighted, sir." The waiter gave a deferential bow as he backed away from the table.

"No wonder you act so spoiled in school," Molly blurted. "When you come here people wait on you hand and foot!" As soon as she realized how she'd sounded, Molly clapped a hand over her mouth, horrified. But the words were already out.

"I can't believe I said that. I'm sorry, Andrew," Molly apologized.

Andrew was quiet for a moment. Then a grin spread slowly across his face. "It's okay. You're right. I do get spoiled here."

Molly sighed and leaned into her crushed velvet chair. She looked at the dimly lit room with its crystal chandeliers, heavily curtained walls, and thick oak furniture. "It's so beautiful. I wish I worked in a place like this." A tinge of bitterness crept into Molly's voice. "It's nothing like the Walters Family Restaurant."

"Things are better at Walters, aren't they? Now that Mr. Walters has left?" Darby referred to Molly's former boss. He was the dreadful man who'd been guilty of sexually harassing Molly.

"Oh, it's much better now. Sometimes, though, if I see a man coming around the corner into the kitchen, I still tense up because it reminds me of how Mr. Walters used to sneak up behind me.

"The new owners are careful to make sure nothing like that happens again. The food is better too." Molly eyed the lavish dessert cart, which the waiter had pushed to their table. "But I'm sure it's not as good as this."

"Tonight our dessert specials are New York style cheesecake, with your choice of chocolate sauce or strawberries," the waiter intoned. "We have carrot cake, chocolate mousse, Black Forest cake, rhubarb and strawberry pie, lemon sorbet, and cherries jubilee."

"Wow!" Molly stared at the cart.

"What do you recommend, Andrew?" Darby asked.

"Definitely the cheesecake. That's my mom's specialty. She makes it personally because she doesn't think anyone else can do it as well."

"Does your mom do all the cooking?" Darby asked after their orders were in.

"When Mom and Dad bought this place, it wasn't much of a restaurant. She and Dad cooked, waited tables, cleaned, did the bookwork ... everything. But that was a long time ago. Now Mom thinks it's fun to come in to make desserts. And Dad's here every evening. He prefers to seat people himself. He thinks his customers like special attention from the owner of the restaurant."

"Do you want to take over the restaurant someday?" Darby asked, taking a bite of the creamy cheesecake drizzled with warm chocolate sauce.

It was easy to talk to Andrew tonight. Some of his cocky brashness had slipped away, revealing a gentler, more introspective person.

"I don't know. I don't really see myself in the restaurant business. The hours are too long. It's difficult to maintain a staff, and I've watched how my parents had to work to build this place. I don't think I have that kind of dedication."

Normally Molly would have chided him about being too lazy to take on a challenge, but tonight she kept her opinion to herself. Instead, she announced, "I think I'm going to burst. Do you see any cheesecake coming out of my ears?"

Jake ate his last sliver of cheesecake, closed his eyes, and gave a blissful shudder. "You're right, Andrew. That's the best I've ever eaten."

"This was a great idea. I haven't felt this relaxed in days. Ever since . . ." Darby's voice trailed away.

" . . . ever since the stabbing, you mean."

"I didn't even want to say it," Darby admitted. "I hate to bring the ugly subject up. Ever since that incident, it seems so much has changed around our school."

"The zero tolerance policy gives me the creeps," Molly said.

"You're not planning to bring a gun to school, are you?"

"No, but it makes me feel all the adults are looking at us students with suspicion. I feel guilty carrying a nail file in my purse!"

Andrew snorted. "You better not mention to anyone you have that in your purse. You'll probably get expelled."

"Exactly what I mean." Molly wagged her finger in Andrew's face. "All of a sudden harmless little things seem serious. It's as though everyone in authority is *expecting* us to be violent. "It's creepy. Like we're in prison."

"Aren't you exaggerating a little?" Jake asked.

"I understand what Molly is saying," Darby interjected. "I feel the same way, but what else are the school officials supposed to do? It seems strict, but they don't want weapons in school."

"Well, there's strict and then there's *too* strict," Jake said.

"What do you mean?"

"My dad has always carried a pocketknife—to school, to church, to work—wherever he went. He says you never know when there might be something you want to cut or trim. A pocketknife comes in handy. He gave one to me for my birthday. Now I can't carry it any longer because of the zero tolerance rule. I'm *not* going to hurt anyone with that knife, so why can't I carry it?"

"Jake's got a point," Molly said. "What about the knives in the home ec. department kitchens? Are they going to take those out of school too? And we did wood carving in art last year. Pretty hard to carve without knives! "Does this mean art and home ec. are illegal now?"

"Don't be dumb!"

"What's dumb? If we take these rules to their logical conclusions, they sound pretty dumb to me!"

"Shhh. Quit arguing. Here comes Andrew's father. We don't want him to think we were arguing."

"But we *were*!"

"How was dessert?" Mr. Tremaine looked down at the empty plates, scraped clean. "Acceptable, I hope."

"They were great!"

"Good, glad to hear it." Andrew's mother walked up beside her husband. "Did anyone have the cheesecake?"

"All of us."

"Andrew is my most loyal customer." Mrs. Tremaine ruffled her son's hair. She was an attractive woman in her early forties. Tonight she wore her dark hair pulled up into a tight bun, which made her look very exotic and just right for this place.

Andrew's father was tall, slender, and impressive-looking in a dark suit, white shirt, and red tie. Andrew resembled his father, but the older Tremaine had laugh lines radiating from the corners of his eyes. Mr. Tremaine appeared to have a better sense of humor than his son.

"Are you having a nice evening?" Mrs. Tremaine asked.

"Great!" Molly sounded a little surprised. Andrew behaving himself and not being a smart-mouth was shock enough, but to find how genuinely pleasant his parents were was equally disconcerting.

"Do you want your table?" Andrew asked his father.

"Not now. We'll eat when the crowd has thinned a bit."

"We should go anyway." Jake pushed himself away from the table. "Thanks for everything."

"Come back again anytime. We'd love to have you."

They were walking toward the door when Molly put her hand on Andrew's arm. "Wait."

"Did you forget something?" Andrew glanced back at the table the waiters were clearing.

"I just want to say thank you. I had a really nice time, Andrew. Much nicer than I expected." Molly blushed. "In school you can be a real jerk, you know. But you weren't tonight. Not at all. I had fun. Thanks."

Sometimes Molly could make kind comments sound worse than insults, but Andrew didn't seem to mind. He was obviously pleased with himself and with Molly's backhanded compliment.

"Have you seen Andrew today?"

"No, and I'm not sure I want to."

Darby and Molly walked toward the media room after their last class.

"Why?"

"Creepy, disgusting, cocky, man-with-an-attitude Andrew was actually nice last night," Molly said. "I'm afraid to see him again, because if he turns back into his old self I'll be disappointed. And if he's still nice, well . . . that's not good either."

"It isn't?"

"No, because I could actually *like* the other Andrew."

"Is that so bad?"

"It is if you've spent practically your whole life disliking someone. He's confusing me, Darby. What's going on?"

"I think he likes you a lot."

Molly smiled a small Mona-Lisa-like smile. "And Jake is crazy about you."

"Ms. Wright wouldn't be happy with us if she overheard this conversation," Darby reminded her friend.

"You mean because of her 'The media room is no place to find a date for the prom' lecture?"

"Something like that."

"My mom always says a person shouldn't mix business with pleasure," Molly admitted. "But I think it's kind of fun."

The girls were laughing as they entered the media room. The entire staff had gathered and were talking animatedly among themselves, some with hand gestures, others with grimaces and frowns.

"Have you heard?" Sarah greeted them at the door. She rolled her wheelchair close to Molly's leg. Her gentle face appeared worried.

"What's going on?"

"There's a rumor around school that a senior girl was expelled for carrying a concealed weapon."

"You're kidding!" Darby gasped. "That's awful."

"I'll say it is," Sarah agreed.

"What did she have—a gun? A knife?"

"That's what's awful," Sarah said. "She was expelled for having a pair of *scissors* in her book bag.

"Scissors as well as knives, guns, cap guns, and baseball bats are included in the new zero tolerance rule. That's why everyone is upset."

"But, Sarah, we use scissors in school all the time!"

"The board says that if students need scissors they can get them from a teacher. Having them concealed in a book bag constitutes having a weapon."

"Did she pull it out and threaten someone with it?"

"No. A guy who didn't even have permission to be in her locker found it there."

"And I don't suppose he'll get punished for snooping without permission, will he?" Darby asked.

"I doubt it. Everyone is so excited about the new weapons policy that they've forgotten about every other rule they've ever made."

"Who's the girl?" Molly wanted to know.

"Jan Elseth. I don't know her myself," Sarah said, "but I talked to one of her friends right after it happened. Apparently Jan has been making a knitted afghan for an art project. She works on it while riding the bus to and from school. Today she brought not only her knitting needles and yarn but also some scissors because she had to change colors partway through."

"Knitting needles? Why didn't they get her for those?" Molly asked sarcastically. "They're deadly too."

"When the school official saw the scissors—and

I'm sure the knitting needles didn't help any—they immediately expelled her."

"Now what will happen to her?"

"I suppose she'll have to be tutored at home. She can't take part in extracurricular activities and may not be allowed to graduate with the rest of her class."

"All because she was making an afghan? That's ridiculous!"

"So you've heard the news?" Gary walked up to the girls.

"What do you think, Gary? Isn't this incredibly stupid?"

Gary shrugged noncommittally. He and Ms. Wright were usually cautious about taking sides. They preferred to let their students think issues through before they were influenced by adult opinions. "The school officials made a promise to parents that the school would be safe for their children. Once they make a rule they feel obligated to stand by it."

"A girl who wants to knit an afghan doesn't sound like much of a threat to anyone!" Darby exclaimed.

"But if they had to decide who was dangerous and who wasn't on a case-by-case basis, the whole system would get bogged down."

"When they installed the zero tolerance policy, they must have taken out the common sense policy to make room for it." Molly was sarcastic.

"But you take the power out of a rule if you don't enforce it," Gary reminded the girls.

"This is silly. That's not what this rule is all about. It shouldn't hurt good kids who make bad decisions.

It should protect us from those people that might want to hurt us!"

Everyone in the room had stopped talking and was listening to their conversation.

"I agree with Molly," Josh said from across the room. "The zero tolerance policy backfired. Now it's more important than ever we do our story on violence in the schools."

"You're absolutely right." Izzy brought his fist down hard on the desk. "It's time for us to get mad. The rules that are supposed to be protecting us are hurting us. It's time we had a say in how our school is run!"

"I love potato chips."

"Is there any ice cream left in that carton?"

"I want your recipe for chili dogs, Izzy."

"Be quiet! I can't hear the commentator."

Some of the *Live!* cast had gathered at Izzy's house to watch a football game. The crowd was divided fifty-fifty over what was more interesting—the plays on the screen or the food on the coffee table.

"Good game." Izzy punched down the volume when the game was over. "I didn't think they'd pull it off."

"Is it over already?"

"Why are you disappointed, Molly? You haven't watched ten seconds of the game. You've been too busy fooling with the food."

"And I'm still hungry." She plucked a chocolate out of a box of candy. "Anyone want to bite into this for me and see if it's coconut? Ew, I hate coconut."

Molly was sprawled on a large beanbag chair in front of the television. Darby and Izzy had claimed a small love seat, while Julie and Kate were seated on the floor. Sarah's wheelchair stood off to the side. As always, Sarah worried that she might be in the way and had refused to roll her wheelchair center stage where she could see the television more clearly.

Josh and Jake were hunched over a small chess table on the opposite side of the room. Andrew and Shane hovered over Josh's shoulders, coaching him.

"What time is it?" Sarah asked.

"Early. It's only nine. Does anyone want to watch a movie?" Izzy poked at the remote control and raised the volume. Movie clips were already sliding across the screen.

"Here's a movie called *Parker's Revenge*."

"Who's Parker?" Molly asked.

"Why does he want revenge?" Kate wondered aloud.

"We'll have to watch it to find out." Izzy flung himself into the beanbag chair with Molly. "Be quiet and pay attention."

Fifteen minutes into the movie Sarah gave a little squeak of protest.

"What's wrong?" Izzy asked.

"Did you see what he did? He poked his fingers into that other man's eyes!"

"Movie magic. Those fight scenes are no big deal. I've seen how it's done. The fighters stand in just the right places so that when the actors pretend to be fighting, the audience can't see that they're missing each other with their swings." Izzy started making grunting noises from where he sat. "It just looks and sounds awful."

"Now they're having a gunfight!"

"What's this movie supposed to be about anyway?"

"Parker's getting his revenge."

"Watch out, he's pulling a knife!" Julie squealed, already engrossed in the movie.

"How can you stand to watch this?" Darby gasped. "Blood's pouring out of everyone's noses and mouths. People in pain are littered all over the ground. This is terrible!"

Izzy stomped his feet. "It gets rough now."

"Wait a minute." Josh suddenly lost interest in his chess game. "Just wait one little minute."

"What's going on in that head of yours?" Molly asked.

Jake grabbed a pen and note pad from the telephone stand nearby. "Time me," he ordered.

Josh glanced at the second hand on his watch. "Starting now."

"What's he doing?" Kate whispered to Julie.

"Who knows with those clowns?"

"There's a punch."

Jake made a check on a piece of paper. "And another. Two more. One kick. He's pulling a knife. Oh, oh, here we go—stab wounds. One, two, three...."

"I get it," Julie peered intently at the screen. "They're counting acts of violence in this movie."

"There's one now—a hit, a punch, two kicks, another stab wound. Okay, stop."

"That was one minute," Josh announced. "How many acts of violence did you see?"

"Almost thirty."

"It was a fight scene. What else did you expect?" Izzy countered.

"Let's try it again. Find a different station. We'll watch a channel for thirty minutes and count out how many acts of violence we see. There's got to be a correlation here between the amount of violence on TV and the steady rise of violence in our schools."

"Don't take my television programs away from me too," Izzy groaned.

"Quiet, Izzy. Here's a piece of paper. Get some pencils so we can all keep track."

The living room of the Mooney household grew silent except for an occasional exclamation. At the end of thirty minutes they tallied their scores.

"It's incredible." Josh stared at the piece of paper in his hand. "I didn't realize how much physical violence was portrayed on television."

"Maybe we have a bad channel." Izzy began channel surfing with the remote. Every time he punched in a new station another fight scene erupted onto the screen. "Or maybe not. It seems to be everywhere."

"That's exactly the problem," Sarah said. "Violence *is* everywhere. Children who watch TV see adults carrying guns and shooting each other. Little kids aren't able to separate fantasy and reality. They don't realize that television is make-believe."

"So what? Little kids aren't going to find guns to shoot people just because they see it on TV."

"Aren't they?" Sarah challenged. "Whatever you put into your mind is what you get out. A person who spends his time watching violence has to be affected by it."

"Maybe violence *is* everywhere." Even Andrew sounded thoughtful.

"We see so much violence on TV that we don't even notice it anymore," Sarah said. "We're numbed to it—hardened by violence and the suffering it causes."

"I think she's right," Darby rejoined.

"I don't agree. We're seeing violence because we're looking for it," Izzy pointed out. "Any other day we would've flipped through the channels and not even noticed the number of shows that portray abuse or violence."

"That's a pretty drastic statement."

"But it's true." Sarah looked troubled. "My parents and I talked about this last night while we watched the evening news. There was a horrible story on television about starving people. Tiny children were sitting beside their dead mothers, rocking and crying, so dehydrated that tears couldn't even form in their eyes. Suddenly my mother asked, 'Why aren't we all in tears at a sight as pitiful and dreadful as this?'

"I thought about that question all evening. We see violence in television shows and movies, on the streets and in our schools. We watch it on the six-o'clock news. None of it's real to us anymore. We don't allow it to touch us. I should have *cried* for that dying baby and its dead mother, and instead, I didn't feel anything!"

"I don't believe that, Sarah. You cry when somebody slaps a mosquito."

"What we see on television distances us from our

own emotions," Sarah insisted.

"Sarah could be right." Jake tallied up the number of incidents of violence they'd seen on TV in the last half hour. "There're some pretty big numbers here. If we all see as much violence as this indicates, our attitudes must be pretty hardened by now."

"You people get excited about the littlest things," Izzy said. "Have you ever watched a football or soccer game? Now *there's* violence. Does anyone ever get upset by that?"

"No."

"Maybe they should," Kate said.

Izzy gave her a disbelieving stare. "Don't talk crazy in my house!"

Just as Izzy spoke, his little twin sisters walked into the room. Heidi and Rachel were as cute, petite, and sweet as Izzy was large, masculine, and intimidating. The two little girls had Izzy wrapped around their little fingers.

"Hi, girls. Whatcha doing?"

Heidi smiled and dimples tweaked her cheeks. "We want to be with you, Izzy."

"Please?" Rachel added.

"I've got company."

Heidi's dimples deepened, making it impossible for Izzy to send his little sisters away. "Puleeeze."

"Can I sit on your lap, Izzy?" Heidi asked.

"I want to sit there," her sister retorted.

"No, you can't. I'm sitting there."

"I am."

"Me."

"Me."

"Me."

The two little girls started to punch at one another.

"Girls, stop that," Izzy protested. They paid no attention.

Heidi and Rachel fell to the carpeted floor, pummeling each other.

"*I'm* going to sit in his lap, you dog-faced dummy," Heidi screeched.

"*I* want to sit there, Stinky Feet!"

"Leave my brother alone."

"He's my brother too."

The girls were really warming up now. The punches began to sound like they might hurt. Suddenly, Heidi kicked Rachel in the shin.

Rachel rolled on the carpet, screaming and holding her leg.

"You're mean and I hate you. I *hate* you," Rachel clung to her leg and rocked back and forth on the floor.

Shocked, Izzy sprang to his feet and towered over the two little girls.

"Stop it, both of you!" he roared. His voice was so loud, his anger so unexpected, that Rachel stopped crying. She rubbed her leg with one hand and put the thumb of the other into her mouth.

"What do you two think you're doing?"

"We want to sit on your lap, Izzy."

"I was first."

"Uh, uh. Me."

Izzy held up a hand to silence them both.

"Why would little kids want to act the way you two are acting?"

Heidi looked surprised by the question. "*Everybody* acts this way, Izzy."

Izzy, who was obviously warming up for a good lecture, was struck dumb at his sister's response.

"What did you say?"

"Everybody fights, Izzy. That's how we do it in school."

"*That's* where you learned to act like little wild animals?"

Heidi stared at her brother as if he'd lost his mind.

"Nobody in this house behaves that way."

"We saw two ladies do it on TV. Didn't we, Rachel?"

Izzy's jaw dropped.

"That's right, Izzy. They were fighting over a man. They wanted to sit on his lap too."

Izzy was stunned into silence.

"They started hitting each other." Rachel started making wild swings to indicate how the women had behaved.

Heidi giggled and covered her mouth with her hands.

"They even fell into the water. Don't you remember? They were fighting by a swimming pool. It was really funny."

The little girls started to imitate what they had seen on television.

As Izzy separated them he was visibly upset. "I don't care what you saw on TV. That is not acceptable behavior in this house from my sisters."

"Are you mad at us?"

"I'm not exactly mad at you, but I don't like the

way you behaved. I don't ever want you to do it again. If you want to sit on my lap, you'll take turns or I'll hold you both, but you'll never fight about it again. Is that understood?"

The little girls nodded, their curls bouncing.

"Now I want you both to go to bed."

"But, Izzy, we want to be with you."

Izzy shook his head stubbornly. "Not after the way you two behaved."

"Are we being punished?"

"I want you to learn a lesson. No more fighting. Have you got it?"

"Not even in school?" Heidi asked.

"Not even in school."

"That's going to be hard," Rachel said.

"I don't care. There are two of you. If everyone else wants to fight, play with each other. Now go to bed."

Heidi's lower lip trembled. "Good-night, Izzy. We didn't mean to make you mad."

After the girls had disappeared upstairs, Izzy paced around the room like a very large lion in a very small cage. "That's it. That's absolutely it. No more. End. *Finis*. My mind is made up."

"What are you talking about, Izz?" Jake asked quietly.

"Something's got to be done about all this violence in society." Izzy pointed a trembling finger toward the stairs. "If the twins are learning it and finding it acceptable, the next thing I know, my own grandmother will be punching the carry-out boy at the grocery store if he doesn't bag the vegetables just right." Izzy flung himself onto the couch and crossed his arms over his thick chest. "Sarah's right. We've started to take violence in society for granted. Until I saw my little sisters acting out what they've seen on TV, I'd have told you that violence on television wasn't dangerous." Izzy ran his fingers through his short, rumpled hair. "I was wrong."

"So what are you going to do about it?"

Everyone had almost forgotten Shane was present. Until he'd started working with *Live!*, Shane had never hung out with any of the people in the room. Even now, he always seemed to be observing, never participating.

"What are you going to do about it?" Shane challenged again. "Shove someone? Shoot someone? Get rid of violence by pounding someone in the head until they listen?"

Izzy flexed and unflexed his hands at Shane's words. "I sounded pretty riled up, huh?"

"That's the problem. Our first reaction when we feel anger is to punch someone out or slam a door."

"But I've gotta do *something*."

"Why? Do you think you can change the world? Who do you think you are anyway?"

"Shane's right. We can't fix violence with violence," Molly said. "There's already enough of it around."

An odd, defeated expression flitted across Izzy's features.

"This is a real downer." Molly looked glum. "It's hopeless! How can we change the attitudes of a whole society? We're probably going to become more and more violent until we blow each other up or beat each other senseless."

"I don't agree, Molly. I can't. That would mean giving up. It would mean that I believe there can't be a better world for me and my sisters than there is right now."

"We're just kids, Izzy. Don't forget that. What can we do?"

"Molly's right, Izz. We don't have any power," Kate commented.

"I'm going to do *something*," Izzy muttered to himself, ignoring the rest of the conversation.

"I think you're wrong, Kate," Darby pointed out.

Kate looked up sharply. She didn't like to be criticized.

"We're just kids, but we do have power. We have the *Live! From Brentwood High* show. That gives us the opportunity to make a difference, at least in our own school and community."

"Too hard," Kate said pessimistically. "Definitely too hard."

"I'm going to do something," Izzy said again, louder this time. "I *have* to do *something*!"

CHAPTER **5**

LIVE FROM BRENTWOOD HIGH

"What do you think? Is it me?" Darby turned so that Sarah could see the embroidered back of the jean jacket she was wearing. Price tags dangled off the collar and rustled as she postured.

"Too tacky. Get the plain one."

"But I feel like being daring."

"Have you looked at the price tag? No one should be *that* daring."

Darby dropped her arms and allowed the jacket to slide into Sarah's lap. "Don't you ever just go crazy and do something impractical?"

Sarah tapped the arm of her wheelchair decorated with silver foil and purple streamers. A sign saying, "Want to drag race?" hung from the back. "You call this practical?"

"I suppose you expend all your creative juices on your buggy. Sorry. I forgot."

"Good. I like it when people can forget I'm in this thing. It makes me feel as though they know *me* and not my chair."

"Is that a problem?" Darby shrugged into her own jacket and returned the other to a hanger.

"How long did it take you to forget I was 'the girl in the wheelchair' and start thinking of me as 'Sarah'?"

"A while," Darby admitted. "I guess I didn't realize what a barrier it could be."

"There are all kinds of barriers. Josh and I have talked about it a lot. He says the color of his skin is just as big a roadblock to making new friends for him as my chair is for me. People look at skin color or metal wheels and forget that there's a real person encased inside."

"Then I'm lucky. I've discovered the real Sarah and Josh—they're great people." Darby took the handgrips to Sarah's chair and maneuvered her between the racks of clothes to a wide aisle. "That's the best part of the *Live!* experience—meeting and working with the staff. I'm even getting used to Andrew Tremaine!"

"Andrew's not so bad as long as you ignore the fact that he's vain, conceited—and probably very insecure."

"Insecure? Are we talking about the same Andrew?"

"I've got a theory. . . ." Sarah was famous around the media room for her theories. She spent a great deal of time watching people and trying to figure them out. "If Andrew were *really* secure, he wouldn't try to keep proving how wonderful or wealthy or handsome he is. He wouldn't care. I think we should treat Andrew with more compassion. . . ."

Sarah snapped her fingers. "I almost forgot! One

of my dad's friends was accidently shot in the arm last night!"

"Here? In Brentwood?"

"He'd returned unexpectedly early from a business trip out of state. He'd planned to surprise his family so he didn't let them know he was coming. When he arrived, it was late and the house was locked. Since he didn't have his key for the front door, he went through a garage door at the back of the house. His fifteen-year-old son heard the commotion and thought someone was breaking into the house, so he grabbed his dad's gun. When the father walked into the kitchen, his son shot him."

"That's horrible! Will he be all right?"

"Yes. They were lucky. It was a superficial wound. The one who's really suffering is the son. He can't get over the fact that he almost killed his own father.

"My dad's very upset about it," Sarah continued. "He thinks people are *more* apt to be hurt by guns if they keep one in their own homes for protection.

"According to Dad, bullets can travel through walls. If you shot at an intruder and missed your target, you could accidentally hit someone sitting in the next room. Dad says if you want protection, you should get a big dog."

"Why is it that every time we begin to research a topic for *Live!* we think it's going to be easy—and once we get really involved we find that it's complex and frustrating instead?"

"'Cause it's like life?" Sarah's laughter sounded like bells as she looked into Darby's disgruntled face. "Ms. Wright never promised us this would be easy!

She only promised it would be interesting."

"Well, it *is* that . . ." A loud yelp made Darby look up from the handgrips of Sarah's chair.

"Izzy, what are you doing here? And what are you yelling about?"

"You ran over my foot!"

"You must have stuck it under the wheel. You weren't there a second ago."

"Don't act so happy to see me. I might feel loved."

"*I* love you, Izz." His sister Heidi threw her arms around one of Izzy's thighs and rested her head against his jeans.

"Thanks, punk." His look softened as he gazed at his sister.

"We're running errands for my grandmother," he explained. "Heidi wanted to come along and. . . ." Izzy glanced downward as his little sister pulled on the pocket of his jeans. "Don't, Heidi. I'm talking to my friends."

"We've been trying on jackets," Darby explained.

"But she can't decide on one," Sarah added.

"How long have you been out here . . . Heidi! Quit pulling on me!" Izzy glared insincerely at the little girl. He looked as ferocious as a pet bunny. Heidi continued to tug on his pant leg.

Finally Izzy reached down and lifted the child into the air and settled her in his arms. "What *is* it? Can't you see we're talking?"

"I want to go to the video arcade."

"I know. I said I'd take you there when we were done with our errands."

"I want to go now." Heidi pressed the palms of her

hands against Izzy's cheeks and bestowed a little kiss on his nose. "Please?"

"Awww, Heidi, don't do that! You know how I hate it when you do that!"

"Tough guy," Darby commented.

Izzy skewered her with a dirty look. His weakness for his little sisters was well known.

"Please, Izzy. You said I could play one game. Then I'll be good."

"You'd better or I'll tell Mom you want your hair cut like mine."

Heidi clapped her hands to her head and squealed. Then she squirmed out of Izzy's arms and held out her hand. "I'll show you where it is."

"As if I didn't know," Izzy muttered.

"We'll come with you," Sarah offered. "We can talk while Heidi plays her game."

They followed the confident little girl through a maze of shops to a darkened room lit only by the garish lights of video games. Blazes of red, gold, green, and yellow split the dimness. Electronic sounds bleeped and buzzed around them. The room was disconcerting with its black walls and flashing lights. At either side of the arched entry doors were large gargoyles with sharp white plaster teeth and lolling red tongues.

They all blinked owlishly as their eyes became accustomed to the dimly lit arcade.

"There's Raymond Martin!" Sarah pointed toward a tall, thin boy in a black leather jacket. "He's in my English class. He always sits in back and never says anything. I think his nickname is Toad. In fact, there are three guys from that class here. I wish I knew their names."

"Be glad you don't," Izzy advised. "Most of the guys who hang around here are losers. Who else would spend their money on video games?"

"Your little sister, for one."

Heidi had dragged a chair halfway across the room, placed it at the front of a machine, and crawled up to work the controls. She looked as though she'd done it before.

Izzy blushed. "I take them here for a treat once in a while, that's all. They're little kids who love games. What can I say?"

Just then Shane Donahue entered the arcade and crossed the room toward them. His swaggering walk spoke volumes about Shane's personality. Nothing and no one would get in his way.

"Slumming?" he asked as he reached them.

Izzy dropped some quarters into Heidi's hand before answering. "A treat for my little sister. What's your excuse?"

"Research," Shane answered enigmatically.

Shane didn't travel in the mainstream of high-school students. He rode his motorcycle too fast, knew too many people who'd had run-ins with the police, and never smiled when he could sneer. Still, sometimes, when he let his guard down, Shane could seem almost friendly and vulnerable. He was a puzzling, complex equation.

"Are you a fan?" Sarah gestured toward the video games.

"Not really. Waste of time." Shane propped himself against the side of the game called "Blood Avengers."

What'd you think of that Sox game last night?" Izzy asked.

While the guys were debating the merits of stealing second base, Darby and Sarah roamed through the darkened room to the buzzes, whirs, and chimes of the machines. A tall boy in baggy shorts and a decrepit T-shirt slammed his palm into a machine as they passed.

"I thought I had it this time!" He aimed a vicious kick at the base of the machine before turning away.

"This certainly brings out the best in people," Sarah commented sarcastically. "Must have something to do with standing in the dark trying to make cartoon figures on a screen behave the way you want them to behave."

"To each his own, I guess. Let's see how Heidi's doing."

Izzy's little sister was still on her chair in front of the flashing lights. Her little fingers worked diligently over the controls. Occasionally her curls would bob when she jumped up and down with excitement.

Darby studied the screen. A series of kick-boxers danced and parried on the screen. Intently Heidi maneuvered them with her controls. Suddenly a new boxer appeared on the screen, this one waving a large sabre over his head.

"Oh no!" Heidi squealed. "Not him!" Heads began rolling as the armed figure kicked and parried his way down the line of fighters. Animated blood poured from the open neck wounds of the beheaded figures.

"Heidi, what's going on?" Sarah sounded alarmed.

"I'm losing. I did something wrong and conjured up the Evil Warrior. Now he's killing all my men. I have to get him."

"Get who?" Izzy and Shane joined Sarah and Darby.

"Have you ever actually *looked* at what your sister is playing?" Darby asked. "I've never seen anything quite so gory."

Izzy peered at the screen. It took only a moment for him to assess the bloody battlefield now depicted. The Evil Warrior was winning. "What's the point here?"

"Nice game you let your sister play, Izz-man," Shane said dryly. "The point of this game is to dismember the opponent before he dismembers you. See all the video blood? Your little sister is getting slaughtered."

A horrified expression seeped across Izzy's face. In one swift movement, he scooped Heidi off her chair and stalked into the hallway. Heidi's wails of protest echoed off the walls of the arcade.

"What'd you do that for, Izzy? I could have won. I know it!"

"Is that the game you always play when you come here?"

"You let us, Izzy. You didn't say we couldn't. I want my game!"

Izzy's fuzzy hair practically trembled with agitation. "No way. I didn't even know they had that kind of violent garbage in there. You're going home right now."

"Nooooooo!"

Tears, sobs, and wails were of no effect. Izzy tucked Heidi in the crook of his arm and headed off. Then he stopped and turned to the threesome he'd left behind. "Meet me at the coffee shop in the east wing in twenty minutes. We need to talk." Without another word Izzy and Heidi disappeared into the crowded hallway.

———

"He's late." Darby looked at her watch. They'd been waiting for Izzy for over half an hour.

"It probably took him longer to get home than he'd thought."

"And to calm down his little sister. I've never seen Izzy like that before. Usually those girls can run all over him."

"Izzy's indulgent, all right, but he'd never do anything to hurt them. He adores them. Seeing his little sister dismembering people probably sent him over the top."

Before they could say more, Izzy appeared, looking even more upset than before. He threw himself into the booth with such force that Darby grabbed for the water glasses on the table to keep them from toppling.

A waitress appeared before Izzy had time to speak. "Ready to order?"

"Don't give him anything with caffeine in it," Shane advised. "He's wired enough as it is."

"A malt. Chocolate. Fries—large. And ice water." Izzy barked out his order like a military sergeant.

When the waitress left, Sarah put her hand on Izzy's wrist. "How's Heidi?"

"Furious. She says she's never—ever—going to forgive me for not letting her finish her game."

"That will last until morning; no longer," Sarah assured him.

"She couldn't quit talking about that stupid video game! 'Izzy, I cut his head off,'" he mimicked. "'Izzy, did you see the blood come out?'

"All she and Rachel have ever played is dolls and house. Now she's into dismemberment!"

"Don't take it so hard. Heidi doesn't understand what she's saying. Those are just cartoon characters to her."

"But if she can accept blood and gore and decapitation so easily with them, won't that affect how she sees *real* people suffering?"

"That's a pretty big jump, Izzy. . . ."

"I think he's right." They all turned to look at Sarah. "It's just what we discussed earlier. Every night we see suffering somewhere in the world—starving children, mass graves, hideous crimes. And do we get all upset? Not really. We see so much that we distance ourselves from the pain of those people. We don't let them become 'real' to us. Accepting violence—any violence, even video games—hardens us to suffering around us."

Izzy's malt had arrived and he was staring menacingly into the creamy recesses of the glass. "First the television and now this. All this violence has got to stop. When it starts to change my little sisters . . ."

He looked up with uncharacteristic fire in his eyes.

"What are we going to do about it?"

Shane, Darby, and Sarah stared at Izzy in bewilderment.

"You want *us* to stop violence? Single-handedly?" Shane finally asked. "You don't expect much, do you?"

"We need solutions!" Izzy hammered his fist against the table, demonstrating his frustration and feeling of helplessness. "Violence isn't something out there, or somewhere else. It's here. In Brentwood. On our TV screens, video games, and movies, in our schools . . ." Izzy's jaw hardened. "And I don't like what's going on. After all, I have my little sisters to think of."

"So this is what it's like to see a mother bear protect her cubs," Sarah mused. "Or in this case, a *brother* bear!"

"I can hardly wait to finish our survey," Izzy muttered. "Then we'll have some concrete numbers. Adults love surveys. Once we have that in hand, we might have some influence. Maybe it will make someone listen to us."

"I don't think all the surveys in the world will make a difference until people begin to realize that change comes from the inside," Sarah said softly. "Both violence and peace come from in here." She tapped her chest.

"That's easy for you to say," Shane muttered. "There's nothing you need to change about yourself. You're perfect."

Sarah looked startled. "Me?" Her laughter rang out in the coffee shop until Shane glanced around, embarrassed. "Shane Donahue, are you trying to flatter me?"

Shane blushed a deep, dark red. "No. It's true."

"Perfectly Prissy, you mean? I've heard all the nicknames I've been given." Sarah was blunt and matter-of-fact. "Miss Goody-Two-Shoes? Missionary Mary?"

"That's not what I meant!"

"I know that. I also know a lot of people wonder why I act so cheerful when I'm trapped in this." Sarah patted her hand on the arm of her wheelchair.

"Well, I *haven't* always been cheerful. And I *did* have to change myself—a lot. After the accident, I was very bitter. I carried a knot of resentment, envy, and hatred inside myself that almost choked me to death. I wanted to be like other kids. Instead, my life was defined by where my chair could go and the few people who were willing to look past it to really see *me*."

"But you're not that way now," Izzy pointed out.

"I finally got smart. It took me a long time to realize that even though I didn't have control over my legs—the *outside* of me—any longer, I *did* have control over my *inside*. Once I chose to be happy—in spite of the chair—I changed. It was like being freed from prison. I don't have to be free of the chair to be free in my mind or spirit. That's what I mean about changing the inside of a person first.

"Trying to change someone's 'look' without changing their attitude is like putting paint on a building that's about to fall down. There's a verse in the Bible that talks about this exactly."

"Of course there is." Shane rolled his eyes and curled his lip, demonstrating his disinterest in biblical anything.

Sarah cheerfully ignored him. "It says in Matthew 23:27, 'How terrible for you, teachers of the law and Pharisees. You are hypocrites! You are like tombs that are painted white. Outside, those tombs look fine. But inside, they are full of the bones of dead people, and all kinds of unclean things are there.' "

"Gross!" Izzy yelped.

"That's just what I've been saying—until people change their *hearts*, all the money or laws in the world won't help."

"We can't forget attitudes need changing right along with rules and regulations," Darby concluded.

Izzy swigged down the last of his malt and stuffed the remainder of his fries into his mouth. "I'd better go home and check on Heidi. If she'll speak to me, I want to have a talk with her."

They'd barely left the coffee shop when they ran into Josh and Dan Travers. Dan and Josh often played racquetball together. Dan was short and muscular, a sharp contrast to Josh's tall, slender form.

Josh and Dan were staring at a display of rifles in the window of a sporting goods store.

"Shopping?" Izzy tilted his head toward the guns.

"What would I do with one of those, other than shoot myself in the leg?" Josh joked.

"Ever thought of carrying one?" Shane's question startled them.

"Me?" Josh paused and cleared his throat. "Maybe."

Only Shane did not seem surprised.

"I held one once," Josh said softly. "A kid who used to live in my neighborhood was trying to sell it. I think even he was surprised that I looked at it. I know *I* was."

Josh held out his hand and stared at it in bemusement. "It felt different than I thought it would. Heavier. Colder. Powerful. I didn't know then that a piece of metal could change a person, but I realize now that it could—easily."

"But why would you want a gun?"

"Don't worry," Josh looked into Sarah's horrified face. "I was never really serious. I wouldn't dare."

"Dare? You'd be the dangerous one if you had a gun."

"Exactly. I'd be the one making the decisions. Being in control might feel good sometimes—when someone is calling me a nigger or threatening to hurt me because I'm black. But what if I was wrong? What if there was no disrespect intended? What if I 'protected' myself and killed someone?" Josh shook his head. "It's not for me. I see why kids crave guns. It's power and control they want. A way to make sense out of a life that seems totally senseless. But as long as kids have guns instead of self-esteem, they're going to hurt each other.

"Just once, when a bunch of kids tried to gang up on me, I wished I had some protection. Fortunately, I came to my senses and realized that if I'd had a gun, people really could have gotten hurt. Guess I'd watched too much television and decided I could play hero—*dead* hero, probably."

"It's everywhere!" Izzy muttered. "Even *Josh*."

"We've got to get Izzy home," Darby explained. "He's had a bad afternoon."

"We're going too." Josh gestured in the direction of the video arcade. "We're parked out there."

As they walked past the arcade, the three boys from Brentwood High that they'd seen earlier stepped into the hallway, blocking their progress.

"Here are the snobs from the media class," one sneered. His hair was long and unwashed. "Slumming with the rest of us peons?"

"Maybe they want to do a report on us," another suggested. He had an unlit cigarette dangling from the corner of his mouth.

"Maybe we could be movie stars." The third was a burly boy with a T-shirt that strained across his chest. "I could be Tom Cruise." He turned. "Right, Dopey? I mean, *Darby*."

Darby and Sarah glanced around for a mall security guard, but there was none in sight.

"We don't want you coming here anymore," the burly boy said. "Stay off our turf."

"It's a free country." Shane appeared unshaken by the encounter. "Mall's free too."

"You wimps can *shop* all you want. Just don't come near the arcade. That's *our* place."

"The owner might be interested in hearing that. I'll bet he thought it was *his* place." Shane obviously enjoyed egging them on.

"We heard your next story is on violence in schools and society. Maybe we should teach you what violence really is. You might not be so interested in asking questions anymore." The long-haired one reached out and gave Josh, who had remained silent, a shove.

Josh staggered backward, caught off balance by the unexpected push. His fists curled next to his sides, but he didn't swing.

"Coward-boy," the aggressor jeered. "Can't even defend himself."

"Against what?" It was Shane again. "He didn't have any bug spray along and that's the only thing that would get rid of you."

The boy's eyes narrowed, but once again he chose not to respond to Shane's taunts. Shane would tolerate little and the three boys knew it. His muscles were tightly coiled, ready to spring into action. His knees were loose and bent, his fingers twitching slightly. He was itching for a fight—and their tormenters were beginning to realize it.

"Just stay away from the arcade. And make sure you don't wreck things for us."

"Make you stop picking on people, you mean? Force bullies off the streets? That *would* be a shame."

The large boy's eyes glittered. "Just make sure that Brentwood High's school board doesn't decide to make any more rules. In fact, maybe that fancy-shmancy media club can get the no coat policy changed."

"And the zero tolerance rule!" the unwashed one added. "We don't like it."

"Maybe we should get a bathing rule passed instead," Shane countered.

"Shane!" Sarah gasped. "Don't . . ."

But it was too late for warnings. A knife had already appeared in the boy's hand. The metal glinted dully in the fluorescent light of the hall. He took one step toward Shane.

Suddenly Shane erupted in a frenzy of action. His leg came up and he kicked the knife out of his attacker's hand. It clattered to the floor and spun across the tiles until it stopped at the feet of a security guard who had appeared out of nowhere. The guard put the toe of his shoe on the blade of the knife while two others grabbed the three boys by their collars and led them away.

"You kids will have to answer a few questions," the remaining guards said. "We've been waiting a long time to get something on those three. Fighting with a knife should be enough to get them out of here permanently."

Shane nodded dully. He was pale, as though he were finally feeling the effects of the past few moments.

It was a subdued group that made its way to the mall offices for questioning.

CHAPTER 6

LIVE
FROM BRENTWOOD HIGH

"Are you okay?" Izzy peered at Darby as she sat on the couch in his living room. Sarah was across from her and Shane slouched in a chair nearby. They'd all retreated there as soon as the security people at the mall had said they could leave.

"I guess so."

"You look a little pale."

"You're surprised? After what happened at the mall?"

"Security knew we had nothing to do with it. They've been watching those three guys for weeks. We just had the bad luck of being there when they wanted to fight."

"Shane could have been *stabbed*!"

"Not likely." Shane shifted in his seat but never lost his boneless, relaxed look. "I've got good reflexes. Besides, I've done some fighting myself." He glanced at Sarah. "Not lately, of course."

"How am I going to tell my parents I was almost in a brawl at the mall?" Darby moaned.

"Tell the truth," Sarah suggested. "It wasn't our

fault. The one who will be difficult to tell is Ms. Wright."

Izzy whistled through his teeth. "I never even thought about her. She'll *freak* when she hears they were threatening us because of the *Live!* story."

"Do you think she'll make us stop working on it?" Sarah worried. "Now it's more important than ever that we continue. We've seen firsthand how quickly and senselessly violence can erupt."

"We'll find out soon enough." Izzy peeked through the curtains to see who was ringing the doorbell. "Gary's here."

Gary Richmond bolted into the room. "Are you guys all right?"

"Sure. Fine. But how . . ."

"I play racquetball with a guy who works security part time at the mall. He called to tell me some of our kids got in a mix-up today. It didn't take me long to figure out who it was. Are you *sure* you're okay?"

"Somebody drew a knife. Shane kicked it out of his hand. He was awesome. Security was right there. No big deal." Izzy nonchalantly summed up the afternoon.

"My buddy said it was a little more complicated than that. They've been watching that arcade for weeks, expecting trouble. How'd you manage to get right into the middle of it?"

Gary's expression grew grim as the story spilled out. He was positively thunderous looking when they were done. "That's it. No more. We can't have you kids risking your necks for a story. I'll talk to Rosie and—"

"But, Gary! We weren't risking our necks. We were at the mall. We were in the arcade watching Izzy's little sister, not doing research. It's not our fault those guys thought we were doing some big exposé on them!"

"Besides, the story is more important than ever—now we know how close to home it touches."

Gary hesitated. "That's true, but . . ."

"Ms. Wright would agree with us, I know she would!"

"Tomorrow Rosie and I will discuss what should be done next."

"You've got to let us continue, Gary. You went to the Gulf knowing it was dangerous. You were in Bosnia when it wasn't safe. This is nothing like the risks you've taken. This story is too important to ignore."

Gary was visibly weakening, but still unwilling to push the incident under the rug.

"Let's watch the early news," Izzy suggested, eager to change the subject. "It never hurts to watch some good examples in newscasting."

Gary didn't argue as the voice of Anna Leemon of Channel 9 news filled the room.

"In a tragic shooting incident on the outskirts of Brentwood this afternoon, a teenager has been severely injured. . . ."

"Turn it up, Izz," Shane commanded.

"A gunfight that erupted between two seventeen-year-olds in north Brentwood has resulted in a serious spinal injury to one of the two young men. He is paralyzed and fighting for his life in Brentwood General Hospital.

"Witnesses at the scene say the disagreement started over a jacket worn by the injured party, which the other young man claimed to be his own. Police are still sorting out the details."

"Over a stupid jacket?" Izzy growled. "Why didn't he just hand it over and—" He was interrupted by a whimpering cry in the other corner of the room.

Gary was on his knees beside Sarah's wheelchair, stroking her hair out of her eyes and gripping her hand tightly as she sobbed.

Izzy and Darby exchanged a confused look at Sarah's sobs.

Gary didn't try to talk her out of her tears but let them flow.

Finally, she snuffled and rubbed at one eye with a balled fist. "Sorry about that."

"Are you okay?" Gary asked softly.

"I guess so. I'm just not very good at handling the news that someone might be paralyzed—even a total stranger. It brought back this flood of memories . . ."

"That's understandable."

" . . . my accident, the day they told me I'd never walk again, the fear. . . . I wish I could tell that boy I made it and that he can too."

"Maybe someday you will. Who knows?"

"Even then I wanted to turn my accident into something *good*." Sarah's fingers gripped the armrest of her chair. "But what good can ever come of this?"

It was the first time any of them had seen the despair or realized the enormity of Sarah's loss.

"You'll find it."

Sarah studied Gary intently, tears still drying on

her cheeks. "You really think so?"

"Positive. I'm a good observer of people. I read personalities pretty well. After all, I've had a lot of experience. You're unique, Sarah. One-of-a-kind. There's a strength in you that I don't see in just anyone. I don't know where it comes from or how you got it, but it's there—and it's going to work for you. I'd guarantee it."

A beautiful smile split Sarah's face and she touched a tentative finger to Gary's cheek. "I think that's one of the nicest things anyone has ever said to me. Thank you."

She scrubbed away the tears still lingering on her cheeks. "Now I feel silly. I'm sorry for being such a baby."

"Pretty tough baby if you ask me." The respect in Shane's voice was undeniable.

Izzy expelled a gusty sigh and a loud burp. Everyone burst out laughing as the emotional moment shattered.

"This day has been too much for me," Darby began. "I think I'll go home and—" She was interrupted by Anna Leemon's words.

"As a tie-in to tonight's shooting story, we're speaking to Doctor Randolph Guester, Chief Administrator of Brentwood General." The doctor flashed onto the screen. He was an intense-looking sandy-haired man with glasses propped above his eyebrows on the prominent shelf of his forehead. He looked thoughtful, reliable, and troubled.

"Doctor Guester, have you seen an increase in the number of gunshot victims treated at Brentwood

General in the past few years?"

"Unfortunately, yes. Even so, we've been fortunate here in Brentwood. The increase has been gradual and has not kept up with national statistics. Guns and violence are a growing part of our nation's health care crisis. Guns—and the terrible things they can do to a human body—will ultimately put a tremendous strain on our health care budget."

"Can you elaborate on that?"

"Injuries sustained in a shooting are usually quite traumatic. They often involve several organs or, as in this case, the spine. There is no 'band-aid' treatment that can fix these problems. It takes time, money, staff . . ." The doctor's voice trailed off. He was visibly upset. It took him a moment to compose himself to continue.

"What's most frustrating is that these injuries are avoidable—*preventable!* Bullets aren't viruses or bacteria. They're man-made and man-inflicted! We've had to tell people to quit smoking. Now do we have to tell them to quit shooting each other? Shouldn't people know better?"

"Thank you, Doctor Guester. And now back to the news desk. . . ."

Izzy catapulted to his feet. "There's another angle for our story! Sure, violence is bad. Sure, guns do damage. But how much damage? Everyone covers the shooting—no one ever tells the story of the *recovery*. No one talks about the billions of dollars it takes to keep shooting victims alive.

"People don't seem to worry about the human factor like they do the economic factor. Maybe this is one way to convince people that violence is out of control. If people think with their wallets, not their hearts, then let's hit them where it hurts—their pocketbooks. If we continue to let violence run rampant, then we're going to have to decide who'll pay the costs of keeping victims alive."

"Maybe people will say 'Let shooting victims die.'"

Sarah gasped at Shane's shocking comment. "You don't mean that! Numbers are one thing. Human beings are another. If you were the victim wouldn't *you* want every effort made to save you no matter what the cost? We shouldn't be trying to play God with the lives of others!"

Shane opened his hands in a gesture of surrender. "There you have it. Both sides of the argument—the emotional and the financial."

"Shane Donahue!" Sarah chided. "You just wanted to start an argument."

"That's our goal, isn't it? To make people think, talk, even argue about violence, until they hash out a solution."

"I think it's the bullets," Izzy muttered.

Everyone stared at him as though he'd lost his mind.

"Of course it's the bullets, you goof-ball! Guns would be harmless without them!"

"Exactly. That's why we should control the sale of bullets. Make them so expensive or tax them so much that no one could buy them! Then we could use that money to pay for the injuries caused by guns."

"Get real, Izz-man!"

"Actually, he's got a point," Gary interjected. "There was an idea put before Congress to put a huge tax on brass cartridges—the hollow point ones that explode and ricochet off body parts causing major damage."

"Why does anyone even *make* bullets that do that?" Darby sighed. "It doesn't make me very proud to be a human being. We aren't very kind to one another."

"But we can learn," Sarah added. "I know we can."

They all sat quietly dwelling on their private thoughts. If *Live! From Brentwood High* had done nothing else, it had taught them all how complicated life could be.

CHAPTER 7

LIVE

FROM BRENTWOOD HIGH

"Now what?" Shane growled to Sarah as he entered the school counseling center.

Izzy and Darby were perched on an uncomfortable-looking couch. All three wore expressions indicating they expected a jolt of electricity to travel through their chairs at any moment.

"I don't know," Darby said. "I just got a message to come here to talk to a counselor."

"Me too," Sarah said. "What do you think it's about?"

"Since it's the four of us who were involved in the incident at the mall yesterday," Darby deduced, "I have a feeling it has to do with that."

"How does anyone at the school even know about that, unless . . ."

Before they could say more, the Brentwood High guidance counselor came out of his office to greet them.

"Hello, my name is Mr. Ricco. I apologize for pulling you out of your first-period classes, but I felt it was important that I meet with you this morning. Please come in."

Reluctantly Darby wheeled Sarah's wheelchair into the office. They all took places across from Mr. Ricco's large desk.

"As I'm sure you've figured out by now," Mr. Ricco began, "Gary Richmond asked me to talk to you about what happened yesterday at the mall. He felt it was important that you be able to express your questions, doubts, or fears."

"I'd like to say something," Sarah volunteered. "It freaked me out last night as I was thinking about what happened. I've always thought of the mall as a *safe* place. It's the first place my mother let me go alone with my friends. Everyone seems so pleasant and respectable at the mall. It's not the kind of place where fights and shootings should happen. Yesterday changed how I will think about it forever. What's going wrong, Mr. Ricco?"

"Good question, Sarah. I've been asking myself the same. Kids have an in-your-face attitude these days. They're more willing to stand up to aggression, more willing to fight. While not backing down from a confrontation can be admirable, fighting is not."

"Why is it happening?"

"It's not just children and teenagers, Sarah. It's everyone. We've become a very angry society. Adults are guilty too. Sometimes things seem to be too hard to talk about, to articulate, so they use fists instead. Sometimes kids fight because it's what they see at home. If parents fight, kids will follow the same pattern."

"But not all parents fight."

"Of course not, but sometimes they're guilty of 'benign neglect.'"

"What's that?"

"Not spending enough time with their children— setting rules but not being home to enforce them, or simply neglecting to talk to their children. And, of course, we all know there is far too much violence in the media."

"That's for sure!" Izzy agreed. Everyone knew he was thinking of his little sisters.

"So what are you supposed to do about it?" Shane was slouched low in his chair eyeing the counselor with something close to disdain. "How are you supposed to fix it . . . fix *us*?"

"I can't fix you. I can only help you to work through any questions you might have."

"And what are you doing about everybody else?"

Mr. Ricco tapped a pencil against the top of his desk. "The most important thing I can do is teach students how to deal with anger without resorting to violence. I need to show them how to work through problems with words, not fists."

"Good luck." Shane's words dripped with cynicism.

"Perhaps we could do something," Sarah said.

"We *want* to do something," Darby said. "Most of the solutions to violence that we've been talking about are things kids can't change. Shane, Jake, Sarah, and I are all on the *Live! From Brentwood High* staff. We have access to a television show that will appear throughout our entire school. Isn't there *something* we can do?"

Mr. Ricco frowned thoughtfully. "That's a very interesting concept. Have you considered creating a youth task force?"

"Task forces are chosen by government agencies to do research on a topic and then make recommendations," Izzy said, dredging up some of the trivia his mind held. "How could we do that?"

"There's no reason that you can't create your own."

"But who'd read anything that *we* put together?" Sarah wondered.

"Lots of people in this city—especially if it were done thoroughly and well. Adults are always trying to understand youth. I don't see how a well-planned study with recommendations could be ignored. It could be sent to school principals, legislators, and anyone who has an interest in violence in the schools."

"This sounds like extra credit time to me," Shane commented dryly.

"Do you actually think the state legislators would look at something from a bunch of kids like us?"

"They need to hear your voices and opinions," Mr. Ricco said confidently. "I have a college friend who is a state legislator. If you choose to pursue this avenue, I'll run it by him and see what he has to say. I'm confident that he would be impressed with a group of young people with vision, energy, and concern for the future."

"Let's do it!" Sarah's eyes had brightened considerably. "I don't like feeling helpless. I've had enough of that in my life already. We're already doing research for the television show. We are almost done with the study we started. Why not make it work double duty?"

"I agree with Sarah," Darby said. "Besides, I think it would be interesting. What do you think, Shane?"

Shane shrugged nonchalantly. "Whatever."

"I don't think it's enough." Izzy frowned, lines of concern etching his wide brow.

"Not enough?" Sarah asked. "Sounds like quite a bit to me."

"It's fine to do research and to ask questions. We need to understand what kids think about violence in today's world, but the fact is that it still doesn't feel like we're *doing* anything.

"We almost saw someone murdered yesterday. One of us could have been the victim. Besides, we know that my little sister turned into some sort of weird monster over a video arcade game. What we're talking about isn't enough. I want to do more!"

Izzy paced back and forth across the room. Sarah and Darby stared at him in surprise. Even Shane raised one eyebrow.

"Don't you see it? Can't you understand?"

"See what, Izz-man?"

"The hopelessness of it all! I don't want my little sisters' minds messed up or my friends murdered.

"No one got hurt yesterday, but it could have happened. Then what? One of us could have been a statistic. We've got to stop thinking of violence in terms of numbers and start thinking of it in terms of people."

Mr. Ricco glanced at his watch. "We still have

some time left in this hour. Would you be willing to stay and discuss your feelings about yesterday's incident while your friends return to class?"

"You think I'm a nut case, don't you?" Izzy demanded. "That's why you want me to stay and you want to send everybody else back to class."

"Hardly that, Isador. You're a sensitive and intense young man who is concerned for his family and school. I respect those feelings and think we should talk about them."

"He *does* think I'm a nut case!" Izzy sank into a chair.

"Should we go now, Mr. Ricco?" Darby asked.

The counselor nodded. "Thanks for stopping by. I'm keeping this afternoon open. If any of you would like to talk to me privately, please let the secretary know."

"I don't think that will be necessary," Darby said. "I feel a lot better. Really, I do."

"Me too," Sarah chimed in.

Mr. Ricco looked at Shane.

He shrugged casually. "I'm cool. Don't worry."

Darby, Sarah, and Shane regrouped in the hallway.

"I've never seen Izzy like this before!" Sarah exclaimed. "He's scaring me."

"It was the thing with his little sister," Darby said. "Izzy adores those two little girls."

"He didn't seem so upset yesterday," Sarah pointed out. "I suppose he's had all night to think about it. I know I certainly didn't sleep very well."

"Neither did I," Darby admitted. "Shane, what do you think?"

"I'm a little worried about the Izz-man too. He's not acting like himself."

"I know this is meddling," Darby began, "but maybe we should talk to Gary."

"That's exactly what I'm thinking!" Sarah exclaimed. "Gary and Izzy get along really well. And Gary's seen a lot. Maybe he has some ideas on how we could help Izzy."

Nothing more was said at that moment, but a pact had been made. Shane, Darby, and Sarah would do anything they could to help their friend.

CHAPTER 8

LIVE

FROM BRENTWOOD HIGH

Gary looked up from the book he was reading as Shane, Darby, and Sarah entered the media room.

"What are you guys doing here? Don't you have class?"

"Not for thirty minutes yet. We were called into Mr. Ricco's office this morning. He told us you'd recommended that we visit with him."

"And now you're here as a lynch mob to string me up for interfering in your lives?"

"No, it's okay, I guess. He was very nice. He had some good ideas. Even one we can use for the *Live!* story."

Gary looked relieved. "I was hoping it would work out that way. I know from personal experience that it's not a good idea to keep things inside too long. They can fester and build up until you have a real explosion on your hands."

"That's what we're here to talk to you about—an explosion, or at least a potential one."

"Where's Izzy?" Gary asked sharply.

"He's still with Mr. Ricco. That's why we came now. We wanted to let you know how upset Izzy is by what happened. He could easily have handled the incident with the knife if it hadn't been for that junk with his little sister. . . ."

Gary closed the book, ready to listen.

———

"Nervous?" Sarah asked when she met Darby in the hallway the next morning.

"A little. I feel crummy—like I've cheated on a friend of mine."

"Don't think of it that way, Darby."

"Maybe we shouldn't have told Gary how upset Izzy is. Izzy might think we're butting into his private life."

"I don't agree," Sarah said. "I know firsthand how frustrating it is to see your world spiral out of control and not know what to do about it.

"Izzy is seeing bogeymen everywhere, threats to his little sisters. You know what a softhearted teddy bear he is. Izzy is accustomed to protecting those girls, and for the first time, he's realized he can't protect them from absolutely everything. Besides, Gary was glad that we told him."

"What can he do about it?" Darby asked. "I was awake half the night thinking about it. I can't think of one thing that Gary can do to improve this situation."

"Have a little faith, Darby," Sarah challenged.

"Faith. Right. That's easy for *you* to say. If Gary can make Izzy feel better about himself and things right now, he's a miracle worker."

The girls entered the media room. It was unusually subdued, caused no doubt by the black cloud that seemed to surround Izzy.

He looked glum, as if he'd discovered his shoelaces were tied together as he'd fallen flat on his face. Jake was making a vain attempt at a conversation. Izzy responded in monosyllables and grunts.

Ms. Wright breezed into the room in a flurry of floral perfume. "Hello, hello, hello. How is everyone today? She dropped her large leather bag onto the desk. Her gaze rested momentarily on Izzy before drifting over the rest of the class.

"I know you're all anticipating learning about key-to-fill light ratio and cross-keying lights."

The class groaned.

"I'm sorry to disappoint you, but there's been a change in the lesson plan. Gary is taking over our class today."

Little mutters of surprise erupted around the room.

Gary meandered to the front of the class looking disreputable as usual. His jeans were worn and his boots looked as though they'd walked many miles. His ponytail was freshly combed, however, and pulled tightly away from his face.

"I'd like you to get out paper and pen. We're going to do a writing exercise."

"You've got to be kidding," Andrew sneered. "How juvenile can you get?"

"You don't know what it is, Andrew. How can you decide you don't like it already?"

"Writing exercises are for seventh graders."

"Not this one," Gary assured him.

When everyone had notebooks out and pens poised, Gary cleared his throat.

"Now I want each of you to write your own obituary."

There was a stunned silence in the room.

"That's what people write about you in the paper after you die!"

"Exactly. Here's an example." Gary locked eyes on Andrew. "Andrew Tremaine, 1900 Exeter Lane, died Monday at Brentwood General Hospital after a long illness."

"Hey," Andrew complained. He shut his mouth when the others in the classroom glared at him.

"As I was saying," Gary continued. "Andrew Tremaine, son of Ethan and Greta Tremaine, graduated from Brentwood High School and Harvard School of Medicine. Married to the former Molly Ashton . . ."

"No way!" Molly protested as the class giggled.

" . . . Tremaine is survived by his wife and three children, Andrew Junior, Ethan II, and Molly Junior, and sixteen grandchildren."

"As if I'd ever name a kid Molly Junior!"

"Sixteen? What are my kids, crazy?"

Gary ignored Andrew and Molly to continue. "Tremaine, who owned the franchise for the twelve hundred Figaro's restaurants around the nation . . ."

"Awright!"

" . . . devoted the latter part of his life to the cooking school he founded. Figaro's became famous for its fabulous seafood because of Tremaine's demands for high quality and superb taste. Tremaine was seventy-six years old at the time of his death."

"That's not so bad," Andrew muttered. "I thought I had to write an obituary that had me kicking the bucket *today*."

"If you don't shut up, I'm going to kick your bucket," Molly threatened.

"Since when did you want to pay attention in class, Molly?"

"What's the point of writing Andrew's obituary if he's not dead yet?" Molly gave Andrew a look of saccharin sweetness which hinted that if he didn't shape up, his demise might come earlier than expected.

"Write these obituaries from the perspective of the *end* of your life. You are currently looking forward to long, productive lives.

"For today, I want you to think about the other end of your life. Imagine you've lived sixty or seventy years; that you've pursued your dreams, fulfilled all the goals you set for yourself. Imagine that there is just enough time left to sum up your life in the three or four brief paragraphs that will appear in the newspaper in your hometown."

"This is depressing," Julie muttered.

Gary ignored Julie's comment. "While you are writing, ask yourself a few questions. What would you like your contribution to be?"

"Contribution? I don't get it," Kate said.

"The things you've given to your community and to your nation. For what would you like to be remembered?"

"I'd like to be remembered for not finishing this stupid assignment," Andrew said.

Gary looked at him. "Are you proud of that?"

"Not exactly." Andrew squirmed under Gary's scrutiny. "I still don't get it."

"Violence has touched close to home lately. Several of you have asked me if there is something that *Live! From Brentwood High* could do or say that would help to curb the violence that we're experiencing. It's a valid question. What can *we* do to change the world around us?"

"Fine. But how will writing obituaries make a difference?"

"Would all of you be willing to work for a better future for yourselves and your children? One that would be safe for everyone? Would you be willing to work toward a society where criminals and victims are few and far between?"

Every head in the room nodded.

"Good. That means that each of you has a vision for the future. Am I correct?"

Heads nodded again.

"What are some things you'd like to see in the future?"

"I'd like to see a future where the stores in the mall didn't have to have those clunky alarms snapped to all the clothes," Julie said. "You know, the ones that can't be removed and an alarm goes off if you try to leave the store. I hate trying on clothes with those things on. They make you look absolutely obese."

"I'd like it if stores didn't have all those mirrors hanging from the ceilings to watch for shoplifters," Kate added.

She patted her hair. "They always make you look so dowdy."

Sam Jenkins raised his hand. "I'd like a world in which we didn't need burglar alarms on cars or removable cassette players. I don't like having to worry about my car in the parking lot."

"And I'd like a world without kidnappers. That way you'd never have to see those pictures of missing children on post office walls and on the backs of milk cartons."

"Excellent! That's exactly what I want." Gary nodded enthusiastically with each contribution to this future vision he was attempting to create. "Do each of you have an image of the kind of world you've been describing?"

"It's safe, clean, and pretty," Sarah offered. "A place I'd like to live."

"Exactly. Keep these thoughts in mind while you pick up those pens and write your obituaries. Tell me, by way of your obituary, how *you* fit into your vision of the future."

"I still don't get it." Andrew tossed his pen in the air.

"Your head is so thick it could shield kryptonite," Kate told him.

Andrew scowled and turned around in his chair, ready to retort.

"Not now, you two," Gary said. "Listen to me. First form your vision of the future. Is it as Sarah said, 'Safe, clean, and pretty'? Do we have homeless people? If not, where are they? Did you take part in a program that provided economical shelter to those in need?

"Do we have racism in the future or are we color-blind? Did your behavior promote racial harmony or racial friction?

"Think about what you want to contribute to that future. Do you want it to be a safe, nurturing, intellectually stimulating world, or do you want it to be one that's spinning wildly out of control?"

"The first, of course."

"Then describe your contribution to that vision of the future in your obituary."

"This is stupid. What good is it going to do?"

"None, unless you take the second step."

"What's that?"

"From now on, when you wake up in the morning think of the world as you'd *like* it to be. Think about yourself and what you'd like *yourself* to be. If you see yourself as a scientist or a doctor, an astronaut or a policeman, every day do something to move yourself a little closer to your goal. In addition, do something to put this world a little closer to the vision you have for it.

"Make up your mind before you get out of bed in the morning that before you go to sleep that night, you will have done something to make this world a better place."

"It's not likely I'll find a cure for cancer," Julie muttered.

"No, but maybe you'll pick up litter in a park or set a good example for a child. Perhaps you'll volunteer to spend an hour reading to a blind person or teaching someone illiterate to read."

"The point being?" Andrew persisted.

"It's a way to take control of your lives. Make a

decision to do something positive for a world that's increasingly negative."

"Do you really think it's possible?" Izzy looked almost hopeful.

"Very few things are accomplished in large steps or in great leaps of inspiration. Do you remember the story of the tortoise and the hare?"

Izzy looked insulted. "Of course."

"Logic tells you that when a rabbit and a turtle race, the rabbit will win. Yet in the fable, the tortoise won the race. Why? Because he kept plugging away, one small step at a time.

"We're turtles, plugging along through our lives. We get through each day and do the best we can. If we do that, day in and day out, without giving up, in the long run it *will* make a difference.

"Reread the obituaries you write for yourselves and then highlight what is most important in them. That is your vision of yourself and of the future. It summarizes what is most important to you."

Gary smiled a wistful, faraway smile. "I'd like to tell you about my mother. She was a great lady, always ready to play. She'd think nothing of leaving a sink full of dishes and a laundry room piled with clothes to go to the beach or have a picnic in the park.

"Once, I asked her about her willingness to spend time with me and my brothers. I said, 'Mom, how can you leave all your work to be with us whenever we ask?'

"She smiled at me and said, 'Gary, when I die I'd like my obituary to read, "She was a good and loving mother"—not—"She kept a very clean house." '

"Each day is important. How you live every day shapes who you are and what you become. Your obituary is a vision of yourself and the future. Remember what you've written and live your lives so that your dreams are reflected there. That's the only way you can actually make a difference in the world."

"I still don't see how I could do much to prevent violence in our country. Politicians are working on it all the time and they're not getting anywhere," Izzy said.

"Maybe not much can be done about large problems in a week, a month, or a year, but in a *lifetime* . . ."

"It actually makes sense," Julie commented. "My dad says we have to look at the big picture. We can't get hung up on day-to-day stuff but have to keep our eyes on our final goal. He says that's what separates a good businessman from a mediocre one."

"Positive goals and attitudes are good for everyone, Izzy," Darby encouraged. "If we only get depressed and discouraged over problems, we'll never solve them."

The new excitement, energy, and inspiration that took over the media room was so intense it was almost tangible. Even Ms. Wright gave Gary a look of admiration.

For a quiet guy, Gary had some really good ideas.

Darby was finishing up some postproduction editing when Jake entered the media room.

"You're still here?"

Darby gestured at the work in front of her. "I could stay all night and not finish everything."

Jake's face split into a grin. "Great, isn't it?"

"I don't think I've ever had so much fun," Darby admitted. "Gary and Ms. Wright are terrific, and the topics we've been covering actually *mean* something. Even the technical stuff with the equipment isn't half bad. Gary's a great teacher."

"There are days I wish I could drop my other classes and just work in the media room," Jake admitted. "But, like Ms. Wright says, without the rest of our education we won't go very far in broadcasting."

"Why did you come back?" Darby wondered.

"To find you. I'm going to visit my sister Kathy at the free clinic where she works. I was wondering if you wanted to come along."

"I'd love to. Ever since I met your sister, I've wanted to ask her more about that place." Darby quickly made up her mind. "Let's go."

The free clinic was located at the north edge of
Brentwood in a part of town that Darby had not often
visited. As the city had grown, north Brentwood had
stagnated. Most of the buildings around the free clinic
looked as if they could use a coat of paint and a little
elbow grease. The clinic itself, however, appeared
fresh and bright, painted a pristine white and
trimmed in black. The bright red letters over the door
read:

Brentwood Free Clinic
All Are Welcome

Inside, the simple tile floor gleamed. The furniture
was old but in good condition. Even the magazines on
the table in the waiting room were neatly arranged.

"This is nice," Darby commented as she looked
around. "I like the pictures on the wall."

"Kathy says they've all been donated by former
patients of the clinic."

"I didn't realize it would be so busy."

There were two families with small children in the
waiting room. The children were well behaved and
playing quietly with the few toys provided by the
clinic. An unkempt old man sat quietly in the corner.
Occasionally he would take a sly peek at the other
people in the waiting room. A woman with a cane and
two teenage girls completed the scene.

It was readily apparent that these people did not
have much money to spend on medical care—or on
anything else.

"Hi there!" Kathy Saunders burst out of the back

room like a whirlwind in a pink tunic. Her hair was piled on top of her head in a tousled bun.

"I'm so glad you came, Darby. Jake said he was going to ask you. We'll start our tour over here."

They followed Kathy through a door into a small room filled with filing cabinets.

"This is our office, such as it is. We could use twice the space, but until the file cabinets reach the ceiling and we need a ladder to get to them, we'll just go with what we have.

"This is Gina, our secretary." Kathy introduced them to a round, motherly woman at a small, untidy desk.

Gina smiled and gave a friendly wave.

"Next door is the lab." Kathy led them into a slightly larger room filled with cabinets, shelving, and several intimidating-looking pieces of equipment.

"There's Marlys, one of our very important lab technicians. Marlys works here one afternoon a week and today's the day," Kathy explained. "She has a full-time job as a lab technician at Brentwood General, but she enjoys coming out here to do some volunteering. Feels good, doesn't it, Mar?"

Marlys's cheeks dimpled as she smiled. "I've never been in a place where patients are so grateful to be poked, prodded, and picked on. Everyone who comes here knows that they wouldn't be able to find good medical care if they had to pay for it. Even pricking a finger and taking blood brings smiles. It's good for my ego."

"Giving to other people makes you feel really good

about yourself," Kathy said. "The people here are so grateful—"

The sound of loud, agitated voices came from the front room, interrupting Kathy midsentence.

"I don't know what's going on out there, but I'd better check." Kathy headed for the waiting room with Jake and Darby close at her heels.

The pristine white waiting room had changed dramatically in the few minutes they'd been gone. A young man, no more than twenty, was sprawled on the floor, his bright red blood staining the tile. Several people hovered over a doctor who had knelt down beside him.

"What happened?"

"Gunshot wound. An ambulance is on the way. We'll do what we can to stabilize him before they come. . . ."

The next few minutes were a flurry of activity, but as soon as the ambulance crew removed the young man from the room a janitor wearing rubber gloves appeared to clean up the floor, and the patients returned to their chairs as though nothing unusual had happened.

"Shall we finish our tour?" Kathy inquired.

Jake and Darby exchanged startled glances.

"You're taking this so calmly!"

"Everyone is acting like this happens every day!"

"Violence in this neighborhood has become more and more commonplace," Kathy said bluntly. "This wasn't the first gunshot victim we've seen, nor will he be the last."

Kathy tilted her head toward the back of the clinic.

"Come with me." They followed her into a small room, obviously used for staff breaks. Kathy poured some thick, black brew out of a coffeepot into three paper cups. "Here, have some of this."

"It looks like it came from the bottom of a river," Jake complained.

"Oh no. What's on the bottom of a river is probably much more tasty. Just drink up. Then we'll talk."

She settled herself at a spindly chrome-legged table and put her feet on a spare chair. "I'm sorry you had to see that incident today, but maybe it's for the best. Jake's told me about your project for *Live! From Brentwood High*, Darby. He says you're looking at violence in schools and in the community. I'm glad. We see far too much of it here. Anybody who can do anything to fight against it is A-OK in my book."

Kathy fingered her coffee cup but did not put it to her lips. "I've been thinking about violence a lot lately myself." She nodded in the direction of the waiting room. "One or two episodes like that in a week and you get scared. Do you know what bothers me most?"

Darby and Jake both shook their heads.

"Violence doesn't hurt just the person toward whom it's directed. Violence creates two kinds of danger."

"Two kinds?" Darby asked.

"One kind is the physical danger," Kathy continued. "The other endangers the soul. Sometimes I'm afraid our entire country is withering emotionally.

"That young man could've bled to death on our waiting room floor. I saw the looks on your faces. You were horrified, but no one on staff was. We've seen it before. Plenty of times. We've hardened ourselves to the sight of suffering. *That's* what scares me. Violence isn't something to which we should become accustomed. We should fight against it every minute of every day."

"You *are* fighting against it," Darby said.

"I hope so. It's the reason I come here even though some days it feels like a hopeless battle. I feel obligated to do *something*.

"At times I ask myself, 'What good does it do? Why do I keep volunteering and coming back? Does anyone care?'"

"You should be writing your obituary," Jake said.

Kathy looked at her brother, startled. "What do you mean by that, young man?"

Jake explained to Kathy the obituary exercise that Gary had them do. "Gary was trying to show us that we shouldn't be discouraged. That we can't look at one day and say, 'Well, I went backward instead of forward. I might as well give up.' We have to keep our eyes set on our goals. We can't let day-to-day things discourage us. Even if nothing happens overnight, things can be changed with time."

"Our friend Sarah says that you have to change the insides of people in order for people to change the outside of things," Darby added. "She says a person's heart has to be good and kind in order for someone to be genuinely good and kind to others. And she says the only way *that* can happen is if God's involved."

"Sarah is a Christian," Jake explained. "She talks like that a lot."

Kathy nodded thoughtfully. "I'm impressed.

Sounds as though you have some pretty solid thinkers to work with on staff at *Live! From Brentwood High.* Maybe your story *can* make a difference. I hope so— I've seen what it's like to work in the trenches. We need all the help we can get."

CHAPTER 10

LIVE

FROM BRENTWOOD HIGH

"I've got it!" Izzy tore into the media room as though a herd of stampeding buffalo were close on his heels. Few in the room even acknowledged his dramatic entrance. By now, the *Live!* staff had grown accustomed to Izzy's noisy, enthusiastic style.

"Got what, Isador? Your assignment, I hope." Ms. Wright adjusted her reading glasses on the bridge of her nose. "You were in charge of the script for the radio show today, you know."

Izzy fluttered his hand as if to wave away the assignment like it was a pesky fly. "It will be done. I just have a few revisions and five or ten pages left to write."

"Isador Eugene Mooney! We have to have that script by—"

"Gotcha! It's done, Ms. Wright. Don't you have any faith in me?"

Ms. Wright slumped against her desk and fanned herself with a script. "Isador, so far all you've given me is gray hair and wrinkles."

"We've got to build a better trust level, Ms. Wright. My psychology book says . . ."

"Get to your point, Isador." Everyone—including Ms. Wright—knew that allowing Izzy off on a tangent could lead to major distraction for everyone within hearing distance. "What have you got?"

"An angle for this violence thing we're covering. This is big, Ms. Wright. We've *got* to talk about gun control."

"Of course, but that's hardly a cutting-edge idea. Everybody is talking about gun control."

"But from *kids*, Ms. Wright. Especially kids who know about *these*." Izzy waved a sheet of paper under Julie's nose. She reached to push his hand away.

"And what, exactly, do you have there?"

"*A list of parts necessary for building my own machine gun!*"

Now Izzy had everyone's attention.

"I put it together from articles I found in a gun magazine. There are conversion kits for sale too. It's easy to buy the parts to convert a rifle into a machine gun."

"*Any* rifle?"

"No, a certain model. But it's no big deal. All the gun parts necessary are on sale, intended to be used to repair other models. Put them together and—presto!—a machine gun!" Izzy scrunched into a firing position and made rat-a-tat sounds. His body twitched as though his imaginary gun were spewing out rounds of ammunition.

"That's disgusting!"

"You bet it is," Izzy agreed. "Nobody needs a gun that can fire multiple shots with one pull of a trigger."

"Isn't it illegal to have a machine gun—homemade or not?"

"Sure. But the people who put them together aren't all that likely to be using them for legal purposes. It's not the sort of thing you'd take to a Sunday picnic. The point is, because there's no regulation of gun parts that are on sale, it is possible to create a do-it-yourself machine gun."

"Things are more out of hand than I thought," Joshua muttered. "Just the thought of Izzy with a machine gun sends chills down my spine."

"But how much control do we really want?" Andrew wondered. "I mean, it *is* a free country. Maybe our problem is that we don't have enough guns. Should we let people steal our property and shoot at us and not even attempt to defend ourselves?"

"What is with you, Andrew? Do you have to be on the opposite side of *every* question?"

"Leave him alone," Ms. Wright interjected. "Whether you agree with him or not, he's got a point. We quit being journalists once we refuse to see every side of an issue."

"If we regulate everything that has the potential to kill, we'd be regulating cars out of existence too."

"And kitchen knives."

"And the food at the school cafeteria!"

At that moment Kate entered the room, her silky black hair flying around her face, her eyes shining. "There's a protest in the gymnasium! A real, live sit-in! People are sitting all over the floor refusing to move. Teachers are pleading with them but so far no one has budged."

"What's it about?"

"They're protesting the no coat, zero tolerance policies! It started in one of the history classes that was studying nonviolent protest. Cool, huh?"

"News in the making," Josh said. "Can we have excuse slips for our next class, Ms. Wright? We should take a TV camera and a tape recorder down there to cover it."

"Okay, but only if you promise not to join the protest. I need you all for tomorrow's show."

"This is great," Izzy muttered as he gathered equipment. "Why didn't *I* think of it? This will really make our story."

———

Darby, Julie, Kate, and Sarah followed Izzy and Gary down the hallway to the gym. Students had begun to congregate outside the open doors. Inside, a group of thirty or more were sitting on the floor. Some were shooting spitballs through the basketball hoops, others were reading books, most were visiting quietly. Three students walked back and forth near the gym stage carrying signs that read "No More No Coat Policy," "It's a Free Country, Let Us Dress the Way We Choose," and "No Coats? No Way!"

Izzy and Gary immediately began to tape the scene unfolding before them.

Darby and Sarah watched the scene near several teachers who had congregated just inside the gymnasium door.

That is where Ms. Wright found them. "Why aren't you talking to these kids? Discovering their motivation? Their goals? What do they hope to prove with this demonstration?"

"Do you *approve* of this, Ms. Wright? If you do, you're probably the only teacher in the school who does." Darby inclined her head toward the cluster of agitated teachers nearby.

"Maybe we should interview the faculty. It would be good to know how they feel about violence in school. Perhaps the students are right and the danger *is* overrated."

As Darby was speaking, Mr. Wentworth, the school superintendent, walked up to them. "Ms. Wright, could I speak to you a moment?"

"We'll just get going . . ." Darby and Sarah started to move away.

"No. Wait. This involves you too."

"Us?" Sarah and Darby looked bewildered.

"I've called Tom Flanders, an educator and expert in school violence, to speak to our teachers and students. It's obvious that we need help to control what is going on in our school. First, there was the stabbing, then the incident at the mall, and now this protest. We need to understand how each of us can protect ourselves and keep our school safe.

"I think that *Live! From Brentwood High* can play a part in this. I'd like your students to tape an interview with Mr. Flanders to be shown to all classes prior to his personal visit with each class. I want to use the tape as both a tool to impart basic information and also a jumping-off place for discussion. Would that be possible?"

"Consider it done. Right?" Sarah looked hopefully at Ms. Wright.

"Absolutely. When will Mr. Flanders be available to do the taping?"

Mr. Wentworth glanced at the protesting students on the gym floor. "Is tomorrow too soon?"

"Sarah, Darby, will you prepare interview questions? Izzy and Shane can help with the taping. Can you be ready?"

Could they? Sarah and Darby were already on their way out of the gym. There was work to be done.

————

Tom Flanders was an imposing man who stood six feet four inches tall and weighed at least two hundred and fifty pounds. He had a thatch of sandy brown hair, bright blue eyes, and a pleasant smile.

The smile didn't fool anyone on the *Live!* staff, however. When Mr. Flanders talked about school violence, he meant business.

"Is his lavaliere in the right place?" Sarah looked toward the sound booth.

"Sounds fine back here. Adjust yours, Sarah. Move it a little closer to your mouth."

They'd rearranged the news set for the interview. Sarah and Darby sat behind the large desk, which had been turned to face the padded chair where Mr. Flanders sat.

"We'll be taking turns asking questions, Mr. Flanders. We'll be using two cameras, but don't worry about them, just look at us. Are you comfortable?"

"And impressed. This is a very professional operation."

At that moment Josh swung a tripod boom over the desk. "Sorry about the giraffe."

Mr. Flanders looked startled. "Giraffe?"

"It's just another name for the boom," Darby explained. "It works well in a small studio like this one, and because it's on casters it's easy for the boom operator to move. Only problem is that it can't be extended. Move it a little closer, Josh."

"*Very* impressive," Mr. Flanders muttered, but the girls were no longer listening. The show was about to begin.

"Welcome to this special edition of *Live! From Brentwood High*." Sarah smiled brightly into the camera. "Today we're talking with Mr. Tom Flanders."

The camera switched to Darby. "Mr. Flanders, a former high-school teacher and coach, has spent the past three years working with teachers and students in an attempt to find workable solutions to the growing problem of violence in the schools."

Sarah turned to Mr. Flanders. "*Is* violence really the problem the media says it is, or are the problems being overdramatized? And if there is a problem, is it as widespread and pervasive as we've been led to believe?"

"My guess is that almost a fourth of the students in this country have been victims of some sort of violence in school settings."

"Isn't that awfully high?"

"I understand your skepticism, Sarah, but it's

true. I've talked to dozens of students who carry guns and knives to school. These attacks are more apt to occur in large urban schools, often those with lower academic standards. Just because these numbers don't fit the average Brentwood student's experience doesn't mean it isn't happening.

"The most rapid rate of increase of this violence seems to be among male teenagers. Arguments that once might have been settled with fists and angry words are now being settled with knives and guns—often with tragic results."

The lights were already getting warm. Mr. Flanders ran his finger along the inside of his shirt collar.

"If it's as bad as you say it is," Darby said, "what are we going to do next? Or is it already out of control? Has violence got the upper hand?"

"Of course not. We can never give up and allow bad behavior to become acceptable. Neither can we change this trend simply by making tougher laws and putting more and more people in jail."

As Mr. Flanders warmed to his subject he put his elbows on the arm of the chair and leaned forward. "We've got to teach our children that disagreements are to be settled with words and compromise, not fists, knives, or guns. And who's got to do that? Parents and teachers."

"But that's what kids see on television."

"Exactly. That's part of the problem. An action-adventure show in which the hero and villain solve their differences by calmly sitting down to talk them out wouldn't attract many viewers. We've got to give kids—even very young ones—better role models if we're going to expect them to solve their problems civilly. Children *learn* violence. That's one lesson we've got to stop teaching."

"Do you really think teaching children good resolution skills will actually make a difference?" Sarah was playing skeptic today.

"It could—along with the knowledge that if they embrace violence they will pay for it."

"Pay for it how?"

"Fines. Jail. Whatever it takes. Too many kids are getting by without appropriate punishment. As far as I'm concerned, there's *never* a reason to intentionally inflict harm. There should be no more excuses. It shouldn't matter whether a violator comes from a broken home or the wealthiest home in the city. Wrongdoing is just that—doing something *wrong*. There should be no question that violence is not to be tolerated and will be punished appropriately."

"That sounds rather harsh."

"No more harsh than allowing teenagers to kill one another."

"But people won't like the idea of kids being put in jail."

"The punishment doesn't have to be a traditional jail cell. Perhaps group homes where kids have to hold jobs, do community service, pay restitution, and go to counselors. But somehow we do have to send out the message that violence will no longer be tolerated and that those who play, pay."

"Is that your only solution? If not, would you share the others with our audience?"

"Long-term solutions include reducing teen pregnancies."

"Really?" Sarah looked surprised. "How will that help?"

"Parents need to be both financially and emotionally capable of taking care of their children so that they aren't turned onto the streets at such young ages. Children having children only creates more problems.

"While enforcing the rules we set, we also have to show young people that we care—as teachers, as parents, as communities."

"Are you familiar with the survey the *Live!* staff has conducted?" Darby questioned. They'd all been busy feeding the information they'd gathered into the computer.

"Yes. It reflects what I know of society as a whole. There's more anger, more confrontation, less respect for law than there used to be." Mr. Flanders paused. "I'd like to ask *you* a question. What are you going to do with the information you've compiled?"

Darby and Sarah exchanged glances. They weren't supposed to let their guest turn the tables on them, but they were both brimming with the news Ms. Wright had given them just before the taping.

"A student task force has been studying the information and has come up with recommendations of their own. We've been invited to present those ideas to some local government officials who have been working on the violence issue."

Sarah smiled sweetly. "But we're supposed to be interviewing *you*, Mr. Flanders. If you could have one wish granted that would work toward solving the problem of violence, what would that wish be?"

Mr. Flanders lowered his head and stared at his hands for a long moment. The studio was totally silent. Darby heard Izzy scratch his head and shuffle his feet.

Finally Mr. Flanders looked up. "One wish? To repair our families and communities so children would feel as if they belong to someone. And that someone would be disappointed if they broke the law or caused another person harm. Too many kids feel that no one is watching, that no one cares. Kids aren't as likely to act up if they know someone's watching. With the breakdown of families and the transient quality of our neighborhoods, sometimes no one *is* watching—and that's where trouble begins."

Sarah looked into the camera. "*No one is watching.* Can we do something about it? Should we try?

"That is our interview with Mr. Tom Flanders, of the Office for the Study of Teen Violence. Mr. Flanders will be in our school this week to talk to you, so please have your questions and responses for him ready. And thanks for watching this special report from *Live! From Brentwood High.*"

"It's a wrap!" Izzy crowed from the back of the room. "Good job."

Mr. Flanders blinked owlishly and looked around. Darby moved around the desk to shake his hand. "Thank you. That should give everyone something to think about before you come to class. If you'd like to view the tape, we can do it right now—just in case there's something we have to edit out."

"That's not necessary. The interview went very well. I'm impressed. I wasn't sure this was a good idea when Mr. Wentworth suggested it, but now I see that he was right. You do a very professional job."

"We're trying. Ms. Wright and Gary are great teachers."

"Does everyone in this program plan to go into broadcast journalism?"

"Some. Others were hoping for a sluff-off class." Darby grinned. "They didn't find it, though. I've never worked so hard in my life!"

Jake, who had been behind a camera, called to Mr. Flanders. "I was wondering if you could give me your opinion of the protest some of the Brentwood students have launched concerning the no coat and zero tolerance policies."

"It's not surprising. They're reacting to what they see as capricious, nonsensical rules being thrust upon them without good reason. The protest is the result of a communications problem. Perhaps the rules should have been instituted more gradually, with more discussion and explanation. In my experience, high-school students do not like change. They grow very accustomed to the status quo. Thrusting radical change on someone without adequate preparation often results in rebellion. The protest is a problem, but not an insurmountable one. Everyone simply has to talk it out.

"My experience has *also* told me that teenagers are not tyrants. They respond to being treated with respect and dignity. They don't feel there's much respect for them when their clothing is being monitored and rules are being set up for what they can and cannot carry in their book bags. Until they see the logic behind the rules and the necessity for them, they're going to be angry. But once they realize the administration's perspective, I think they'll agree."

"I never thought it would happen," Darby said with a sigh. "Stabbings, protests, security guards in the halls. It makes me sad. Now I can understand why my grandfather keeps talking about 'the good old days.' Around here, the good old days were just last month!"

CHAPTER 11

LIVE FROM BRENTWOOD HIGH

"Again?" Darby groaned. "How many times has that phone rung tonight?"

"No problem." Jake picked up the remote control for the television and started flicking through the channels. "I've been waiting for a chance to see what else is on. This is the most incredibly stupid sitcom I've ever..."

Before Darby had the receiver to her ear, a voice hissed over the line. "Get over here right now!"

"Molly? Is that you?"

"Of course it's me!"

"Why are you whispering?"

"Because he might overhear!"

"Who?"

"Andrew Tremaine. Are you coming? You've got to help me!"

"I don't understand..."

"Andrew stopped by. He's sitting in my living room like he's planning to stay. I don't know what to do with him."

"I've got company. Jake is here."

"Bring him along. Bring your brother along. Bring

your parents if you want! Just get over here. I don't know what to say to Andrew. He looks funny."

"Funny? How?"

"Like he might want to kiss me or something!"

Darby suppressed a giggle. "That *is* a crisis. But what am I supposed to do about it?"

"I think he wants to get something going between us. Me? Can you imagine?"

"It's not so bad. He can be kind of nice if he wants to be."

"I don't care! Come quick—before he tries to put his arm around me!" The phone line went dead.

"What was that about?" Jake punched the mute button on the remote.

"Molly's spazzing. Andrew stopped by and she doesn't want to be alone with him."

"I thought she was starting to think he was okay."

"Me too. But apparently he's moving too fast for her." Darby picked up her jacket. "Do you mind running over there? She seems to think there's safety in numbers."

Jake and Darby were laughing as they rang the doorbell to the Ashton home. It was a simple ranch-style house in a middle-class neighborhood, but the yard was immaculately kept and the older car in the driveway was waxed until it gleamed. Andrew's brand-new Trans Am looked out of place on the driveway beneath a tattered basketball hoop.

The door flew open and an arm snaked out to draw Darby inside.

"You don't have to pull," Darby told Molly, rubbing at her arm. "I didn't plan to stand outside."

"Where's Andrew?" Jake inquired, winking at Molly.

"In the living room. Why don't you go in while Darby and I get some sodas from the kitchen?"

Obediently Jake headed toward the living room while Molly towed Darby in the opposite direction.

"He's after me, Darby, I just know it," Molly complained as she put ice into tall plastic tumblers. "What am I going to do?"

"What do you *want* to do?"

Molly paused. "I don't know! I've always thought Andrew was a selfish, egotistical jerk, but lately he's been pretty nice. Maybe it's an act. Maybe it's a trap. That's it. He's going to make me think he's changed. I'll start to like him and then—Zap!—he'll turn into a creep again. It would be just like him—"

"Aren't you getting worked up over nothing? Maybe Andrew was just bored and wanted company, so he came over."

"Then why didn't he go to your place? Why here?" Molly's hands began to tremble. "Why do I always attract the wrong kind of guys?"

Darby took the soda bottle out of Molly's hand. "That's what this is all about, isn't it? Your self-confidence. Just because the last time you fell for someone it turned into a disaster doesn't mean it will happen again."

"Anything that has to do with Andrew will turn into a disaster," Molly muttered, but her voice had steadied. "Why would he even *want* to be around me?"

"Because you're pretty and funny and interesting?"

"Hah!"

"Because you can make people laugh and because you care about others."

"I doubt Andrew is into any of that."

"Because you're a thick-headed dope?"

"Maybe that's it." Molly's watery smile turned into a grin. She put her arm around Darby. "Thanks. I needed that."

"We all need a reality check once in a while." Darby picked up two glasses. "Let's go see what the guys are doing."

When they reached the living room, Izzy was sitting on the couch with Andrew, and Jake was positioned in a recliner nearby.

"What are you doing here?" Darby asked Izzy.

"Hi to you too."

"You know what I mean. I didn't hear the doorbell."

"Jake saw me coming up the walk." Izzy dug his hand into the bowl of pretzels on the coffee table. "Did you hear the news? Jan Elseth might be reinstated in school."

"The scissor-carrying girl?"

"The board decided that they'd better iron out the bugs before they start expelling students. She gets to come back, but she'll have to be on probation."

"And what happens the next time someone carries a pair of scissors in a bag and forgets it's there?"

"Mr. Wentworth asked us to do a story on Jan for the school paper as a warning to other students. She wants to tell kids what happened to her.

"There will be lists of 'forbidden' items posted at every door. Next time someone gets caught, they want to be sure it's someone who knew the rules and still *intended* to bring a weapon into the school. If this doesn't work, they're installing metal detectors like they use at airport security."

"Progress," Darby said with a sigh. "Sometimes it feels like we're going backward instead of forward."

———

"What've we got?" Ms. Wright glided into the media room, her gauzy India skirt drifting behind her.

"Enough interviews, information, and tape to do a documentary." Izzy stared morosely at the stacks of reports and papers before him. "How are we ever going to sort all this out and edit it down to a manageable show?"

"You should do a *60 Minutes* or *20/20* kind of thing," Molly suggested. "You've done all the research. Now put it together. Don't waste it."

"Yeah. Right. And who'd watch it? I'm not sure even my grandmother would consent. And *she* thinks everything I do is perfect."

"I think everyone would."

"Huh?" Izzy stared at Ms. Wright. "What'd you say?"

"I said I think that everyone would watch it. We've got an hour for the in-school program, and several teachers have requested that it run during their class periods.

"Mr. Flanders is interested in extra copies of the

interview Sarah and Darby did with him. When I told him about the rest of the information you've compiled, he said he'd like to see that on tape too. He thinks it would be a great teaching tool for the schools he visits. He feels it would mean more because the video was done by students rather than adults. He said he might be able to find some distribution through the educational system if the tape appears professionally done. And since that's our goal anyway..."

"Are you serious? He actually *wants* our stuff?"

"To use in other schools?"

"Is there any money in it for us?"

Ms. Wright burst out laughing. "We can always count on you to get to the bottom line, can't we, Shane? There's no money involved, but if you present your findings and the task force's recommendations to the public, I can guarantee that people will sit up and take notice.

"In fact, I just got word today that the school board would like you to present your findings at their next meeting. Mr. Wentworth called to tell me that your student task force recommendations were well received. There's even a letter on the way from one of our congressmen saying thank you for our work!

"And that's not all. Because of the attack in the arcade and several incidents we hadn't even heard about, Brentwood's mayor has formed a committee to look into gang violence. He seems to think that gangs are in their 'infancy' here and that intervention might have some good effect."

"We're making a difference in others' lives!" Sarah

beamed, joy apparent on her features. "We're actually helping others!"

"Yes!" Josh chimed. "We've got people listening to what we say!"

"And you're giddy with power." Gary, who had wandered silently into the room, made the observation with a smile.

"It's not often we get power," Josh pointed out. "Feels good."

"I think we're creating monsters, Rosie."

"As long as they're ethical, moral, conscience-raising, contributing, creative monsters with a sense of justice and purpose, I suppose it's all right."

"Speaking of monsters . . ." Molly muttered as Andrew sauntered into the room.

Everyone burst into laughter. No matter *what* the *Live!* staff did, some things would just never change.

Some of the staff of *Live! From Brentwood High* go undercover to research the discrimination aimed at disabled people—and what they discover leaves them shocked. What's more, Izzy's adventures in baby-sitting almost prove too much even for him. Find out what happens in Book #4 of the *Live! From Brentwood High* series.

A Note From Judy

I'm glad you're reading *Live! From Brentwood High*. I hope I've given you something to think about as well as a story to entertain you. If you feel you have any of the problems that Darby and her friends experience, I encourage you to talk with your parents, a pastor, or a trusted adult friend. There are many people who care about you!

I love to hear from my readers, so if you'd like to receive my newsletter and a bookmark, please send a self-addressed, stamped envelope to:

Judy Baer
Bethany House Publishers
11300 Hampshire Avenue South
Minneapolis, MN 55438

———

Be sure to watch for my newest *Dear Judy . . .* books at your local bookstore. These books are full of questions that you, my readers, have asked in your letters, along with my response. Just about every topic is covered—from dating and romance to friendships and parents. Hope to hear from you soon!

Dear Judy, What's It Like at Your House?
Dear Judy, Did You Ever Like a Boy
  (Who Didn't Like You?)